HALF WILD

HALF WILD

WILD

STORIES

ROBIN MacARTHUR

ecco

An Imprint of HarperCollinsPublishers

HALF WILD. Copyright © 2016 by Robin MacArthur. All rights reserved. Printed in the United States of America. No part of this book may be used or reproduced in any manner whatsoever without written permission except in the case of brief quotations embodied in critical articles and reviews. For information address HarperCollins Publishers, 195 Broadway, New York, NY 10007.

HarperCollins books may be purchased for educational, business, or sales promotional use. For information please email the Special Markets department at SPsales@harpercollins.com.

FIRST EDITION

Designed by Ashley Tucker
Hand lettering by Sara Wood
Title page photograph by PlusONE/Shutterstock, Inc.

Library of Congress Cataloging-in-Publication Data has been applied for.

ISBN 978-0-06-244439-4

16 17 18 19 20   OV/RRD   10 9 8 7 6 5 4 3 2

—

FOR
THE WOMEN WHERE I'M FROM—
AVAH MARGARET,
GAIL MARIE,
AND MARGARET JEAN

—

Listen: you are not yourself, you are crowds of others, you are
as leaky a vessel as was ever made.
—REBECCA SOLNIT, *THE FARAWAY NEARBY*

Then grow wild in the thin grass, over fossil
And nowhere to lie without some animal
To find me.
—SOPHIE CABOT BLACK, ˙HOME˙

CONTENTS

———

ACKNOWLEDGMENTS

Oh, gratitude. To my grandparents, the scientist and the song-catcher, who wed us all to this landscape. To my dad, who took me into the woods when I was young and then took my babies into them thirty years later (for hours at a time) so that I could write this book. To my farming mom, for her intrepid ways and for growing the food I feed my children. To the big-hearted community at Vermont College of Fine Arts, especially my teachers— David Jauss, Laurie Alberts, Jess Row, Larry Sutin, Diane Lefer, Clint McCown, Xu Xi, David Treuer, and Ellen Lesser—who believed in and refined this work. To the editors at the literary journals where these stories first appeared: R. T. Smith at *Shenandoah,* Ronald Spatz at *Alaska Quarterly,* and Barry Wightman and Samantha Kolber at *Hunger Mountain.* To the brilliant friends who have encouraged me to go deeper, and deeper yet: Lauren Markham, Sara Reish Desmond, Miciah Bay Gault, Mika Perrine, and Jennifer Bowen Hicks. To my dear agent, Julia Kenny, without whom this book would be sitting in a box somewhere, housing mice. To the fabulous people at Ecco, who welcomed me onto their ship and gave this work their hours, especially Eleanor Kriseman, Sonya Cheuse, and my astonishingly whip-smart and generous editor, Megan Lynch. To all my friends and loved ones, here and gone, whose smoke winds through these pages. To Ty, my partner in a love supreme, for making the music, for plot-doctoring at all the right times, and for believing in and supporting me, always. And to my children, Avah Margaret and Owen Cricket, loud and luminous, who every day reach for my hand and take to the woods, bounding.

HALF WILD

1

CREEK DIPPERS

"You want to jump in the creek?" my mother asks. It's a Tuesday night in late July and we're on the porch drinking Myers's rum doused with lemonade. She's wearing cut-off cargo pants and a Grateful Dead T-shirt full of holes; her cracked toenails are the chartreuse of limes.

"No," I say, to which she snorts and throws her cigarette butt into the wet grass, where it hisses before losing its flame. Mist rises from the field. Baby grasshoppers pop. Clouds drift.

I don't want to go down to the creek with my mom. Nor do I want to be living here at sixteen in this deciduous/ coniferous northeastern no-man's-land of Vicksburg where we were both born, forty square miles of inter- secting roads, intersecting streams, failing farms, and rocky ledge. Populated by ghosts and animals and lonely women. *Frickin' heaven*, my mom calls these woods.

Heaven: like she'd know. She's thirty-three years old and pocked with life's failures: her sun-lined face and cheaply tattooed arms and soot-lined lungs. My mother has cleaned houses, waitressed, logged, gardened, trained horses, hammered nails, groomed dogs, hung Sheetrock, and killed other people's livestock for a living. It's made her body crooked, wrinkled, callused, bent. But she's a tiger, too. She has a tattoo of a mountain lion on her left thigh that reminds me, every time I see it, of the love-warrior inside her. The one who wanted something other than what she was born with, who nursed me until I was three (*little titty-monkey*), the one who lays her hand on my shoulder when I come home from class and says, "Angel, you be good. You be real good, baby-o."

Angel? Your mother named you Angel?

What is it with us and our mothers? The way we both love and hate them. The way they define ugly and yet we catch their face in our mirror and surprise ourselves with—gladness.

The last mountain lion they saw in our state was in 1883. They shot it in the hills above our town, and now it's stuffed in a museum in Boston, tawny eyes aglow. My mom tells me she'd like to steal that motherfucker someday. Free it from its goddamn stillness. She's only one-sixteenth Abenaki but claims that cat as her spirit animal all the same. And so that tiger tattoo, inked across her bony thigh.

But tonight she's talking about dogs. About how she thinks we should raise them to sell. For money. Always dreaming of money. Always in need of more. She gets up and pours us each another glass; coyotes yip down by the creek: a fresh kill. Her words drift to wolves. "Did I tell you about Alaska," she says, taking a sip, handing me mine.

Yes. She has told me about Alaska. She's been telling me about Alaska my whole life. Roy and a trailer surrounded by wolves, surrounded by pines. The only place she'll ever go other than here.

My mother and I have lived in this house, this hunting cabin on concrete blocks she stuffed with insulation, since before I was born. There's a creek below, a field out front, a gravel road that runs straight for a while, and this porch. This porch. What is it about houses? The way their simplest elements contain who we are, say things for us. I was born on the living room couch, a mattress over a couple of crates. There was blood and my mom's great-aunt Sugar with bundles of herbs and warm, thick hands.

"I think we could make good money raising dogs," my mom says, nodding her head, as if I've agreed. "Half-wolf breeds. Half wild. Big buckeroos. Big stinkin' buckeroos. Don'tcha think, Angel-o?"

She doesn't wait for me to answer.

"Wolves," she says, balancing her wide, bony foot in the air, touching the moon with its silhouette, laughing. "There were goddamn wolves in Alaska."

She's getting drunk, I can tell. I close my eyes and she disappears. I don't want to be a pioneer. I am silently naming the places I might go: Chicago. New Orleans. Amarillo.

We're waiting for the storm, which we can smell coming through the trees. We're waiting for Robbie, her boyfriend with the bad teeth. We are, in some regards, waiting for dawn, or tomorrow, or next year. Leaves shuffle. Milky clouds stream past. The creek calls the water in the clouds home. My mom says it smells like desire and tips her head back, sniffing.

Desire. For a moment I know we both feel it: our shared loneliness. A deer steps into the far edge of the field—stick legs, dark pools of eyes—then turns away into the gray trees.

Objective correlative. I learned about it in my course on twentieth-century American literature. The way we anthropomorphize the world around us. I read Faulkner and Hemingway and Eudora Welty, books by *frickin' dead white folks,* my mother said at the time, reaching for her Pall Malls.

Yes, I didn't say, eyeing the bitter streak of her cancer stick, but those books are beautiful. They make me think of nights like this, on the porch, clouds and crickets and this blue hunger, only they turned it into something other. Took it off the porch and into the air. They got the fuck out of Dodge, those men and those women. An aunt of mine lives alone in West Texas. Another on a mountain north of here. Is this hereditary? Some kind of messed-up, errant gene?

But back to the here, the now.

"Fuck, it's hot. Just a quick dip, Angel-love?" my mother whispers hoarsely, opening her eyes for an instant before closing them again.

I don't respond.

Someday I'll talk about this porch. I'll tell a story about Sue, my mom, weeping or yelling amidst the blackberry canes and fireflies, the wild roses. About the way she drags the TV out here sometimes late at night to watch scenes from the Iraq War: the explosion of far-off bombs, the sad companionship of the box's blue flicker. About how she throws shit at the screen every time George W. Bush's face appears, whispering *Motherfucker*. Or maybe I'll just say "porch." Porch. My mother had a porch, resting on telephone-pole piers, on which she lived.

"Let's go," she says, stubbing her cigarette and downing her rum. Robbie, we both know, will show up soon in his rusted-out plumber's van, shuffle up the steps with a six-pack of beer. There is nothing wrong with Robbie. Absolutely nothing wrong with or extraordinary about Robbie.

We head toward the creek—Silver—its banks lined

with rocks and moss and roots and tangled ferns. We've dammed a spot with logs and sticks and concrete blocks so that there's a three-foot-deep pool of clear running water, a patch of sandy bottom. Not much, but enough on nights like this. We strip. Wade in. Feel the cool climb our shins. The aunt in West Texas lives in a trailer at the edge of town with a view of the Big Bend Mountains, a dog named Peco, and a truck named Rose. What the fuck, I want to say to the blood-dipped moon.

My mother goes first. Butt, chest, shoulders, then flips onto her belly and dips her whole head under. I go next. Underwater you can see the glisten of stones, the toss of ferns (ostrich, lady, wood). My mother's white, magnified body resembles a whale, beached in far-too-shallow water. My own? Downed birch trees? Coiled wire? A deer?

The water is ice-cold, mountain melt from higher ground and deeper springs. I raise my face and look up at the dark sky, peppered with holes.

"Goddamn fucking lovely!" my mother shouts, grinning, stepping out of the water. She rubs herself down with her Grateful Dead T-shirt, slips into her underwear, heads toward the light. "Robbie'll be here soon. You coming, Angel?"

"Nah," I say. "I'll stay." I'm freezing underwater, my body a cube, but diaphanous with stillness. My mother disappears up the footpath, and I dip my face back under, head tipped back like a dolphin, like a bracken fern, like an old wheel, spinning.

I think of those people I will someday give my body to. I think of the girls I go to school with, their normal mothers. I think of these roads, fields, creeks, ephemeral mountain lions.

I stand up in that shallow lit by moonlight and stay there for a moment—naked amidst the eyeless trees—then step out of the water, dry off, and slip into my clothes.

There are voices on the porch. Candlelight, Robbie's van, smoke rising. I'm freezing out in the field, but I'm made of bronze, too. Cast iron in T-shirt and jeans, barefoot and far from pregnant amidst the grasshoppers and trees lit by moon.

What is it about fields? The way they make all directions viable. The way they give houses, porches, voices perspective. The way the word itself—*field*—makes you feel both domesticated and wild, both wolf and human, capable of heading toward that porch with its smoke and laughter, or toward the woods, where you could quietly and, without a sound, start walking.

2

THE HEART OF THE WOODS

My father's a logger, my brother a builder of houses, my husband a real estate man. Our lives are tied to the fate of trees the way some people's are tied to money, others religion. But my father believes there is an insurmountable distinction between logging and real estate. Logging, he says, can be done tastefully, with heart, so that a year later no one knew you were there, so that the trees left standing have a chance to thrive. Real estate, he says, can never be done well. He has called my husband a carpetbagger, a rich bastard, and a flatlander all in the course of an evening, which means he doesn't come to our house anymore. It means when I want to see his glistening angry blue eyes and catch the familiar earthy whiff of hemlock sap and cigarette smoke and clean sweat, I get in my car and come here to the Stonewall on Route 100, where I know he'll be sitting in the afternoon light across from Rita at the far end of the bar, drinking the finest Scotch they carry, the kind they keep in stock just for him.

And I can tell you the name of every other person here as well—Joe Maise, Terry Miner, Rich Miller, Jay Cole Jr. They nod to me as I walk in, these people from my past, but they don't offer to buy me drinks. They all know my husband is the one with the shiny slew of white pickup trucks that all say his name—RON BATES—trucks that drive around these towns buying up cheap and undeveloped acreage, parceling them off into four-acre lots, selling them at a profit. Or if he doesn't sell them, Ron hires my father to clear the land (he still shows up for the cash), my grandfather and cousins and uncles to mill the wood, and my brother to build spec houses on the land: houses that invariably sell. They are good-looking houses for the young professionals who work ten miles downhill in Nelson at the hospital or the nuclear power plant or the car dealerships. We've done well for ourselves—better than the Maises or Miners or Coles—which is why when I enter the bar they simply nod at me, the girl they went to school with, the one with the red hair, the one some of them made out with in the front seats of cars back when we were young.

My father offers to buy me a drink, though, and I accept, even though I live in a six-bedroom house with marble tiles in the front entryway and he lives in the same Tyvek-covered two-room cabin where I was born.

"Sure, Dad," I say, while Rita pours me a glass of Glenlivet and I sit down on a stool next to him, our elbows almost touching. "How are you?"

"Upright and breathing," he mumbles into his glass. His lips turn up in a sly grin. "You, Sally?"

"Good," I lie. "Things are good," scraping the toe of my boot against the barstool rung.

When I was young I was his favorite. "Sally Mae, Sally Mae, prettier than the green of May," he would half shout, half sing when he came home in the evenings in his green Dodge truck. In the summer he would put me on his shoulders and take me out into the woods, teach me the names of trees, how to strip sassafras bark for chewing; in spring, how to tap a maple. "The woods are something to be grateful for, not shit on," my father would say. "So be good to them."

I tried to be.

"You eating well?" I shout into his right ear.

"Oh, yeah."

"Keeping good company?"

"Not good enough till Rita here will come home with me," he says, setting his glass down on the counter with a little click to get Rita's attention, winking at her when he does.

She shakes her head lovingly, an old friend. "Oh, Calvin, go find a woman half your age."

I don't like to admit it, but I'm jealous of Rita each time I come here. Rita, fifty-eight years old, five foot three, 160

ROBIN MACARTHUR

pounds, with undyed hair, is beloved in my father's eyes, while I am nothing but an embarrassment, a sore.

Like my mother. Who hated our house—its outhouse and small rooms and drafty windows and lack of electricity or neighbors. "Woods," my father said, nodding toward them, as if that made us rich. She used to ride in the truck when he delivered wood for the Scandinavian wood stoves of summer people and doctors in Nelson just so she could look at and admire their big, clean houses, their bright lights shining.

But enough of the past. I sip my drink, breathe, pull my shoulders down, look around the dim room: pine walls, wooden booths, neon Miller signs. Behind the bar a ten-point buck stares quietly. To my left a stuffed bobcat leaps out from the wall, amber eyes aflame.

Terry Miner stands up from his end of the bar, goes to the jukebox, and slips two quarters into the slot. Alan Jackson starts to sing. For a moment I watch Terry's skinny jeans, the cracked leather of his boots, and the sun-bleached and thinning waves of his hair—then turn back toward the bar and stare into that buck's still eyes.

The clock says five thirty; Ron will be getting home any moment, which means I should go, heat up last night's dinner in the microwave, open a bottle of Bordeaux, but instead I linger. He will lean in to smell the heat of liquor on my breath and ask where I've been. But so what if I've come to slip momentarily into the old ways of my life, to

12

get a little tipsy and sit by my aging father listening to country tunes. What harm is there in that?

My father orders another drink and pulls another Marlboro out of his pack. I let the secondhand smoke fill my clean lungs; he leans toward me and nods at my glass. "Another?"

I think for a moment of Ron, then catch the glint of that bobcat's eyes on the wall and Terry Miner's body in the corner. "Why not."

"Oh good," he says, facing Rita and grinning. "She is a McLean after all."

"I've always been one," I say, my voice caught in my throat. "Just changed my name. You know that."

"Changed more than that."

"Don't pick a fight with me," I say quietly, sliding my glass toward the edge of the counter so that Rita can see.

How many years will I have to walk this line—trying to prove myself in both worlds I belong to?

"Not the kind of man to pick fights, right, Rita?" My father winks at Rita and nudges me with his elbow. She refills both our glasses, and I wonder how many my father has had already.

"Thank you," I say as she slides my glass across the counter.

Rita nods at me but doesn't smile.

I've disassociated myself from this town in most ways: the car I drive, the clothes I wear, the places my husband and I go for dinner.

You can't get rich in this place without accumulating spite. Ron buys land from old ladies and broke farmers and single women. I work for the business two days a week; it's my job to find out who's having hard times, who's likely to sell. It's my job to go to their houses, knock on their doors, ask sweetly how they are doing. The Coras and Violets and Hazels and Annes.

Like today, at the house of Alice Tucker. A two-hundred-year-old Cape with broken slates and rotten sills sitting on two hundred acres of prime land. She opened the door in a lilac-colored housedress, smiling, her false teeth loose in her mouth. I caught the scent of skin powder and cat litter and wood smoke. She didn't invite me in, so I just stood out there in the driveway in the hard sunlight.

"Alice. It's me, Sally. You know, Calvin's daughter. Sally McLean," I said, catching the soft look of recognition in the impoverished old lady's eyes.

Keep business local, Ron and I say. Keep it in the family. Land isn't something you can hold on to forever. There have always been real estate people, tax sales, down-and-out folks desperate enough to sell. And we give them cash, these old ladies and hard-luck farmers, cash like they've never seen before. Cash they go out and buy new pickups with or double-wides, cash they use to fly themselves to Florida or the Bahamas. I see the smiles on their faces.

"You need help with the car insurance this month?" I shout toward my father. Because of three car accidents in the last two years, his insurance has reached astronomical highs. I don't know why he hasn't yet lost his license. I assume he knew the boy in the cop car who asked him to say the alphabet backward, who declined to smell his breath.

"Nope." My father is clearly embarrassed to be having this conversation here in front of silver-haired Rita, but we have no choice. "Should be fine."

"Well, you know where to call."

"Yep, I do," he mumbles, staring at the bottles behind the bar.

On winter nights when I was young our driveway was impassable, and so he would carry me up the hill on his back, and I have a clear memory of the sound and rhythm of his heavy breathing and regular steps through the snow, of the delirious and sleepy sensation of being transported safely through the dark and cold night. He's the same man, I know, and I'm the same girl, but who is taking care of who has reversed direction.

Terry Miner gets up from his seat and goes back to the jukebox. Again he pulls two quarters out of his front pocket and puts them in the slot. This time Waylon Jennings starts singing about honky-tonk angels in heavenly flight.

"Hah!" My father grunts. "Heaven!"

I smile. He was never one to believe in heaven. When I was eight my mother found religion and tried to change my father's ways, but he refused to go to church. Sunday mornings we would come home, dressed and clean, to find him at the kitchen table or, in summer, in a chair at the edge of the woods, his blue eyes glistening. "How was God?" he would shout to us across the clearing, grinning. My mother would walk stiffly toward the house, refusing to look in his direction, the pressed cotton of her dress swishing against her thighs. My brother and I stood frozen in the clearing, unsure of which way to turn.

When Terry Miner turns back around he catches me looking at him, and I am surprised to find him walking toward me, his hand stretched outward.

"Dance this one?" he says.

I feel my father's and Rita's eyes on me. My palms start to sweat, and I think for a moment of Ron, at home in front of the TV, waiting, but I say yes. Why not? I'm not in these heels, these jeans, this blouse, this bar, for nothing. I think back to a night when we were eighteen, a circle of friends drinking beers by Sunset Lake, of the way I had watched Terry that night, lighting off fireworks at the edge of the shore, of the way I had, some hours later, stripped my clothes off and slipped into that cool, dark water.

We start to dance, and his grip is firm on my arm and lower back. He smells like beer and diesel fumes. Terry is married to Louise, a girl we also went to school with. They have three blond, beautiful children. I close my eyes and will the faces of those children to disappear. But Terry's grip is tight on my arm.

"Heard you went by Alice's place today," he says in my ear. His voice is not friendly.

"Yes," I say.

"She's my great-aunt."

"I know that, Terry."

"I grew up fishing on that land. My boys ride four-wheelers there."

"I didn't know that," I say.

I look up then at his blue eyes ringed with lines, and he nods at me. "Just so you know," he says, his eyes cold.

I look back at him without blinking. "Now I know," I say.

We are quiet for the rest of the dance, our limbs awkwardly colliding, our heads swaying to the three-quarter rhythm. When the song ends he grins at me briefly, then gives my arm a hard pinch. "Always a pleasure," he says, and I nod, and we go back to our places.

My father has turned back toward the bar, though I know that he, like everyone else, was watching us. People don't dance in bars around here. I take another sip of my Scotch.

We're not dumb, Ron and me. We saw early that if you're going to survive in a place like this, it won't be by milking heifers from dawn to dusk or burning your neck all summer trying to grow hay. Trees are what grow here: west of the Connecticut River valley, east of the Adirondacks, in the low, wooded hills of southern Vermont.

They are what pay our dental bills, buy us our pickup trucks, secure the loans on our SUVs.

"Tell you what, Sally," my father says, turning. "You should come back with me tonight. Got something at home to show you."

I haven't been to our old place in years, its half-sided walls, its clearing full of old tires and rusted chairs.

I look down at my hands for an instant, then into the yellow eyes of that dead cat on the wall. I think of Terry Miner's hands on my arms, of the weight I felt there. Of that near bruise humming under the skin. "Okay," I say. "I'll come."

"Rita, one more shot for the road," my father shouts.

Outside I walk toward my Lexus, but my father shakes his head. "Take a ride," he says, so I climb instead into the passenger seat of his twenty-year-old GMC.

He drives fast along the back roads, taking corners too quickly, spinning out on the gravel edge. He passes me a Miller from the well below my seat, and I pop it open, drink. It's not far, I think to myself, watching the blurred trees and beyond them the deep blue fields, and it's not. Soon he's pulling up the dirt track, the truck lurching up the steep bank, and then we are parked in front of his cabin, the place I lived when I was young.

I haven't had this much to drink in I don't know how long, and my head spins, but I feel strangely giddy as well. Ron will be wondering where I am, forehead fur-rowed, and the thought somehow thrills me. *I'm back in the woods, Ron.* The voice in my head is saucy, irreverent, unlike my own. Is it my husband or my dead mother I'm talking to? *Back where I came from. Trash still.*

I think of Alice Tucker's housedress. The paper-thin skin of her arms. I think of that cat's amber eyes on the wall above the bar.

My father opens the kitchen door, and I follow him in-side. There are clothes thrown over the back of the couch, a chainsaw taken apart on the living room rug. He starts toward the back door to take a piss.

"What did you want to show me?" I call out.

"Oh. Yeah. Here. Look at this." He points to a couple of photos tacked to the pine wall above the sink. "Found them in a box."

I've only seen a few photographs from my childhood. Never these. One is of our family sitting in front of this house when my brother and I were young, our dog Tuck by our side. The other is of my parents in a field, my mother's red hair lit by sunlight. Her dress is the color of apricots or poppies; her eyes radiate joy. It's a look I rarely saw there.

"Is that your wedding day?" I call out, but my father's still outside so I have nothing to do but look at her pretty, young face and the quiet hope that is spread out all over it.

"Enough staring at the past," my father shouts as he

steps back inside. He buttons his pants and heads toward the refrigerator. "You can have those. Another?" he asks, handing me a Pabst.

"Yes," I say, feeling something weak overtake me.

"Here then."

I follow my father outside to where he has a couple chairs set up next to each other under the trees. He hands me the can, and I pop the top and take a sip and listen to the robins chattering and the deep, spiraling song of the veery and to my father's heavy breathing and to my own heart beating in my ears. He pulls his pack of Marlboros out of his front pocket and lights a cigarette.

"I'd like one too," I say. I haven't smoked in years, and my father glances at me sideways, his eyebrow raised, then grins and hands me one.

"You sure remind me of your mother," he says, looking upward.

"I do? Why?"

"Never liked the woods."

"She didn't. But I do."

"Hell, never liked anything about the woods at all."

My heart is all cat, squirrel.

"No. But I do."

"You'd think a man could have figured that one out sooner. That woman sure knew what she wanted, didn't she?"

I look at my father and see then that tears have filled

his eyes, a cloudy mess of salty grays and blues that look like riled ocean.

"Yes," I say. "She did." My head is reeling with drink and the bright heat of the last spark of afternoon sun, and I see a single tear drip down his stubbled cheek and rest at the tip of his chin, not falling.

Then he reaches for my hand and takes it in his, and it is as if for a moment I am that girl again—pretty Sally—on his back being carried in snow through the fields of winter. I take a deep breath and feel the last rays of afternoon light on my face and chest and chin, and then he lifts his hand and reaches it across my arm and rests it—and it is here I should stop him, but don't—on my blouse atop my left breast, and for that moment I am overcome with the potent sweetness of his touch and with it, his love. I smell his familiar scent of chain oil and hemlock and smoke and think, in that moment, of those snow-lit fields, that lake water, and of my mother, and her joy, and how little I knew of it, and then he's whispering my mother's name—*Mona*—and that's when I realize where I am, in my drunk father's yard, and who I am, and pull away, not looking at him, and stand up, stumbling toward the edge of the clearing with my can of warm beer.

"Oh shit," I hear him mumble.

In the woods it is already dark with evening shadows, and I'm grateful that I can't make out his face clearly, nor he mine. I set my beer down on a log and make my way

toward the driveway. "I'll see you soon, Dad," I shout
through the dim light, though I wonder how, and where,
and when. He doesn't say anything back, and I'm glad.

I walk the whole way back to the bar, three miles, slipping behind stone walls and trees when cars pass. My feet
burn with blisters and my legs ache, and by the time I
get to my car it is dark, the sky heavy with the absence
of stars, and I am long sober enough to drive, but I don't
go home.

Instead I drive around back roads—Fox, Stark, Sunset Lake, Butterfield—the roads I grew up on, past the
houses where the people I grew up with lived and live. I
pass Alice Tucker's house, and look this time not only at
its falling-in shape, silhouetted against the sky, one light
on in the kitchen window, but also down toward Silver
Creek, where Terry Miner learned to fish when he was
a boy.

One night after my mother and brother and I had
moved into an apartment in Nelson, my father came by.
He knocked at the door and stood out there in the dark
calling our mother's name up toward our windows. *Lock
the doors,* my mother whispered. *And pray for his soul.*
We did. We lay in bed listening to him out there calling
her name—*Mona!*—and singing fragments of old love
songs, once in a while simply howling.

I roll down my window and keep driving, past moonlit trees and fields and open land, the land my husband

wants to buy, the land I could help him buy, the trees that could become lumber, and feel the dangerous and frightening pull of some new, or old, kind of life—drunk, hopeless, pine-pitched—calling.

And then, when it is late, past midnight, I drive north and a little east, and pull up my paved driveway, and turn off my car, and look up at the safe, bright lights of my home. I walk in the front door and close it behind me. Ron is there, rising from the couch and walking toward me, his brow furrowed, his eyes soft with worry.

"Where were you?" he asks quietly.

"Nowhere," I say. "Just my dad's. I was just at my dad's." And then Ron takes me in his pale, thin arms and holds me loosely, and just like that I slip back into the shape of my life. I smell his clean, washed body, and know I will go on buying land and helping cut up and clean up what is wild out there, and old, and unseemly. I close my eyes and know my father will die someday, and with him that wild and unsettling hunger to go deeper, and deeper yet into the heart of the woods.

3

WINGS, 1989

That day in July my mom came out of the house, wiped her soapy hands on her thighs, and told me to get my lazy bum up off the grass and go weed the peas. She wore rolled-up blue jeans, a plaid cotton blouse, and a red bandana that tied her dark hair back from her face. Her toenails were caked with dirt and needed cutting.

"Don't want to," I said. My dad had been gone on a job for a week, and it was just the two of us. In the sun the temperature read ninety; bugs swarmed around my skin and flies landed intermittently on my thighs and knees.

"Katie, how'd you get to be so lazy?" she said, squinting off toward the hills that used to belong to my dad's parents but had since been sold, and then started walking alone through the tall grass down to the garden. I watched her shoulder blades moving under her blouse and went back to the library book I was reading. It was about a girl who lived in a clean house in the suburbs with lots of rooms and windows. The girl wrote stories, and the book was about those stories she wrote and all those windows. I wanted to be like her: unencumbered, surrounded by light. In one story she wrote about girls who turned into birds: hawks and ravens and buzzards and crows. They could fly anywhere they wanted to go. You knew, reading, that the girl who wrote the stories was free, too. You could feel it in your bones. But I couldn't concentrate anymore, with my tired mom walking down to the garden alone.

I felt a trickle of sweat slip down my spine and thought about those weeds—tall, green, stringy—crowding out the tomatoes and peas and carrots and beans. I thought about our basement full of empty canning jars collecting dust and our Datsun with a busted starter. After a few minutes I got up and went down the hill too, knelt in front of the carrots and pigweed. My mom didn't say a thing, just looked at me sideways for a moment and smiled, then went back to the peas.

We lived in a house that didn't have many windows, just a few small double-hungs in each room that we covered with plastic in winter. My dad had built the house when he was twenty: a pine-sided cabin with two bedrooms and a porch and a barn where he had hoped, someday, to keep goats or horses. Now that barn was just a place with no walls where we kept snow tires and broken lawn mowers and old chairs in need of caning.

The weeds were thick and everywhere: pigweed and witchgrass and dandelion. It had rained all of June, and standing water pooled in between the rows and mosquito eggs floated around in the pools. But that day was all sun. My hair fell into my face and stuck to my cheeks, and the thin brown hairs on my legs shone. Wet dirt wedged under my fingernails and made them throb. The skin on my arms and legs burned. My mom's arms were a nice freckled brown, and she didn't sweat. Mine were my dad's: pink and burnable.

"Swing low, sweet chariot," my mom sang, quietly and out of key. She had grown up in a big house in the suburbs, just like the girl in my book, and could have done anything with her life. Back in college she had wanted to be a poet. There were floppy books of poetry stored on a shelf in the corner of her bedroom, collecting dust. Adrienne Rich and Sylvia Plath. There were old lace bras in her underwear drawer that she never wore. I got up and moved to the grassy shade at the edge of the garden. I lay down and closed my eyes and thought about how a Coke or a blue Slush Puppie or a sip of my mom's ice-cold wine would feel on my tongue. I could hear her inching along through the rows. I picked a blade of grass and stuck it between my teeth and nibbled on it, let the bitter taste seep all over, and then I spit it out and just lay there, feeling the cool.

I had the story of how they met like a movie in my mind. My dad had a job at the local college building storage sheds. It was hot and he worked with his shirt off and all the girls hung around, my mom told me, pretending to read near where he cut and hammered boards. But she was the only one to offer him a glass of ice water. He said he'd love one but that swimming was an even better way to cool down. Then he grinned. "You like to swim?"

He took her to a place in the Silver Creek called Indian Love Call and told her it was named that because Indians would bring their girlfriends there. On one side of the river a ledge outcrop rose twenty feet above the water, and they carried their towels up to that rock and looked down. The water bristled with snowmelt, and the boulders flashed silver in the sun. He beat his fists against his chest and made a hooting call meant to imitate an Indian; his voice echoed back. Then he took off all his clothes and leapt into the water. My mom stood there in her jeans and blouse looking down at him. He crowed and hollered and splashed and looked up at her. She laughed. "What you waiting for?" he called out.

"It looks cold!" she shouted above the sound of water hitting stone.

"Fresh!" he yelled, so my mom took off all her clothes and jumped in too. She'd never been naked in front of a man or leapt off a cliff into ice water; she said she knew right then, in midair, that her life would be something entirely different from what she had imagined.

"You all done?" My mom stood up, brushed her dark hair out of her face with the back of her hand, and looked down at me on the grass.

"Yeah. Pooped," I said, so we walked back up to the house together. The sun had settled below the trees, and the sky bloomed tangerine behind the leaves. She was quiet. In one of her not-talking moods. "Speak, woman," my dad would say if he were here, poking her ribs, trying to get her to crack a smile. "We're missing you down here."

She put some rice on the stove and started chopping spinach and peas. Every once in a while she'd glance up at the old-fashioned clock that hung on our wall and made a loud ticking sound I knew so well that sometimes I couldn't hear it when I tried. On top of the clock sat little wooden turtles and rabbits and birds my dad had carved for both of us years ago.

She looked again at the clock. It read seven thirty, which meant my dad should have been back a few hours ago, which meant he and Davie, the guy he built houses with, had either broken down or were smoking a joint at the river.

She licked her dry lips and looked at the door. It had warped over the years and now a half-inch gap of outside light shone between the door and the frame. Once she had asked him to fix it, so he took some duct tape and pasted a strip over the gap. "There," he said, grinning, laying the duct tape on the table. The strip of tape still hung there, half peeled down, the sticky part dull with cobwebs.

My mom turned the tap water on, and the light over the kitchen sink flickered. She had asked him for real electricity too, not the long cord strung from tree to tree through the woods up from his parents' house that made the lights flicker every time she used the blender or ran water. My dad just laughed and left the room when she asked for that.

I heard his truck coming up the driveway and went outside. When I was young we drove that red Ford to Florida and camped in a tent surrounded by pines. We cooked on a Coleman stove, and my mom's skin turned a beautiful brown; there are pictures. There's also a picture I took of the two of them dancing barefoot on the beach at dusk, my mom's neck tipped back, her mouth wide with laughter.

My dad hopped out of the truck and came toward me. "There's my beauty!" he called out, scooping me up and swinging me around in a circle. His eyes were bloodshot and he was grinning. He set me down and looked at the house. "How's Lyn?"

We walked inside together. She didn't look up, just kept chopping her vegetables, the knife making little scratching sounds on the board. "And beauty number two," he said, quiet, breathing.

He went around the counter to where she stood and put his arms around her waist, placed his thumbs on her hip bones. "I said hello, beautiful," he said into her ear. Then he looked at me, his eyes glistening. He was stoned, I could tell. I loved him when he was stoned; he talked to both of us this way. My mom stopped chopping her vegetables and closed her eyes. The cotton of her shirt went up and down with her breath. Then she pushed him away with her elbow. "Go take a shower."

We ate dinner at the table out in the yard: rice and veggies and a can of pintos my mom opened up. She didn't even heat them on the stove, just dumped a pile onto each of our plates. My dad got a six-pack from his truck and opened a bottle and told us about his week. He told my mom this was the biggest house they'd ever built, that he was going to make a profit. "I'll buy you any goddamn thing you want," he said, grinning, leaning over and pinching my thigh.

My mom poured some white wine into a Ball canning jar. She took small sips and squinted out toward the view. She was doing that thing she did, I knew: trying, with her eyes, to make the hills flat, pretty. Turn them into poetry. They used to belong to my dad's parents. Now they were just black silhouettes spotted in ugly houses, the sky behind them the blue of my dad's eyes, and mine.

ROBIN MACARTHUR

He set his beer down and looked at my mom. "Okay few days, Lyn?"

She took another sip of her wine. "It was all right."

Their faces were shadows. My dad leaned down and unlaced his boots, slid his feet out of his boots and socks, rested them up on the bench between us. They were pretty like a woman's: pale from being inside his boots all the time.

My mom got up and cleared the plates and took them into the kitchen. I heard water running and the kitchen light flickered. Mosquitoes swarmed around my head and bit my legs. I let one turn red with blood, and then I swatted it so it left a smear on my thigh.

"Ugly," my dad said, and laughed, but it was an out-of-proportion laugh, like he was laughing at something much funnier or not funny at all. I sat there waiting for another mosquito to land on me and fill up with blood. I thought about the girl in my book and how she didn't think about her parents' spent dreams, or weed their gardens; all she thought about was the people in the stories she wrote and about herself.

"How about you, Katie Belle," my dad whispered. That's what he called me. "Doing okay?"

The back door slammed and I went around the side of the house. My mom was going down the hill to the garden in the near dark. She kneeled by the zucchini this time, pulling more weeds, trying to make things right. It

32

was a losing battle, I knew. I followed and stood quiet in the shadows a few yards away. After a few minutes she stopped weeding and bent over and put her face in her hands. Her shoulders started to shake. I looked at the view and then at my toes and then back at her. The shadows of her shoulder blades started moving around under her skin. The skin of her back stretched out until it was gleaming, nearly translucent. Large pointy things, the length of my legs, began moving around, poking through her ribs and skin.

"Mom," I called out, my voice too loud in that dark.

She looked up at me. Her eyes hazy, viscous, blank. Those things on her back were iridescent, dark feathered wings.

Then a look of recognition passed through her. "Oh. Hi." Those wings disappeared. Stopped pulsing there. She had been crying but she looked beautiful. "Want to help, Kate?"

My heart was electric, but I went and knelt next to her. It was the only thing I knew how to do. We pulled until it was so dark we could no longer tell the difference between one thing and another: unearthing spinach and peas and beans. A firefly flew into her blouse and started blinking in there. She laughed and tugged the cotton away from her chest, and the bug flew out. Then she put her arms around me and held me to her. She smelled like dish soap and earth, but something strange and sour that I'd never smelled before, too. All around us crickets were finding their partners. I thought about my dad up there alone at that table and how I'd always be like him: wingless, from here.

"You cold?" she asked. She started shaking and I could feel those wings again, behind me, trembling below the surface of her skin.

"No," I lied. The night air was warm but I was freezing. Only where she touched me was I warm. Her breath was sour, uneven, scented with wine. On the horizon the moon started to come up through the trees—just a sliver, then disappeared behind the tops of the hemlocks and the pines.

4

MAGGIE IN THE TREES

I can smell Maggie everywhere in here: black coffee, tree bark, skin. I can smell her in the couch cushions in the half-size kitchen, and in the dirty sheets of the bed where she lay down three times one day in August when outside it was near ninety and humid as drink. We were like that then. I would get up and boil water for coffee, thinking the best way to cool down was to start sweating, like caffeine makes me do. Thinking how she and I needed something to get our bodies out of bed, out of the trailer, out into the shadows of the pines where I had set up two lawn chairs and a cooler for beer. From the kitchen I could hear her slipping into jeans, pouring a glass of water; I could feel the tired ache from my balls hanging limp between my legs making me feel exposed and ugly and foolish, too, if there had been anyone else there to see, which there was not. There wasn't anyone except Maggie and me within one-point-two miles, and it was all trees and granite and a steep logging road between here and there.

If anyone had come, it would have been Rich, Maggie's husband and my best friend of thirty years. Rich, who hooked the trailer onto the back of his Ford F-250 and dragged it up the trail behind his house that week in April after Deb left me, recognizing a wounded animal when he saw one. Said, *Pete,* leaning over the hood of his truck. *I been thinking. How 'bout you move onto my place? Give yourself some time to get your feet back under you.* Rich, who said, *We go way back, man. It's the least I can do.*

So I did.

Now I throw a pair of jeans on and pour water from my five-gallon jug into a pan on the stove. My body throbs from beer and an empty stomach and the burning sensation on my skin that has not left me for weeks. I glance out the window—am always glancing out windows. The dawn light is a sheet of orange spreading amidst the trees here on top of the hill, and I think for a moment maybe it's fire—want it to be fire—but it isn't, it's just sun. I pour the hot water through a filter, take my coffee outside, and sit in a lawn chair wet with dew. Maggie: chestnut hair, one blue eye, one brown. *Once I wanted to be a teacher,* she told me. Laughed. *You think I would have made a good teacher?*

Yes.

Ha! She took a sip of her coffee and pinched some leaves between her fingers: little fingers, chewed pink

nails. Streaks of gray in her dark hair. *Never even gradu-
ated from the tenth grade.*

A crow takes flight above me, and I turn my head to
watch it disappear into this hillside—the home of the
headwaters of Silver Creek—Maggie's Mountain, as I
call it, Whiskey Mountain, to others. *You know why it's
called that?*

No.

*Because some poor fella died making moonshine. Went
blind one day; the next he came back for more and died.*
She laughed, that cigarette-worn caw. *Can you imagine?
A place named after that kind of wanting?*

Yes. I think now. Yes I can. Wanting and waiting—
always waiting. For Maggie. For Rich. Every morning—
for days, weeks—waiting for the sound of his truck up the
steep track, his fist on my door, the click of a shotgun behind my head. Waiting for him to come up that path and
tell me to leave, or kill me, or grab me by the nuts and pull.

But as always there is just this light, these birds, this
dew. It soaks through my jeans, and I think for a moment
I am cold, that I will go inside, and then I think of that
river water, translucent and deep, and picture Maggie in it,
a flash of white skin, moving, and I think, *Fuck cold,* and
close my eyes and conjure Maggie: beautiful, sad, drunk
Maggie.

I had heard something rustling in the leaves. A deer, I
thought, after the spikes of June's new grass. The late-

afternoon yard cool and bright, leaves crackling with the first dry heat. I poked my head out the trailer door.

Hi there, Pete. She stood in the clearing in her hiking boots and cut-off shorts, shifting her weight from one leg to the other. Small but strong, tan, those unsettling eyes.

I stepped outside. Mumbled hello.

She asked if she could sit down for a while, and I nodded, so she sat down on a birch log. I went out and reached into the cooler of beer that I kept on the north side of the trailer and pulled out two bottles. I had known Maggie for years, but we'd rarely had a conversation just the two of us. She was Rich's woman: quiet and wild and inscrutable. She took the bottle and tipped her head back for a long drink, closed her eyes.

It's been a while since I've been up here, she said, opening her eyes, looking around.

I nodded.

She turned the bottle around in her small hands, her shoulders bent forward a little. *How you been getting on?* She glanced toward me, then away.

Okay, I guess.

Lost?

I laughed into my bottle. *Yeah.*

What you do all day?

I shrugged. *Read a damn lot. Drink too much beer. I haven't gone back to work.*

No job. That's never good. Her face softened, her eyes flickered with light.

No, I said, watching those eyes, suddenly unsure. *Never good.*

She raised her beer toward me. *Here's to you, Pete,* she said, smiling.

I raised my beer, felt something light and warm rise in my chest. When the bottles were empty she stood, set hers on the step, and brushed off her shorts. *I'm going up to the top of the mountain,* she said, glancing toward the trail.

I sat there looking up at her legs and arms and at the bright sky behind her.

She looked straight at me. *You want to come?*

My eyes hung on her for a second that felt too long. *Yeah,* I said. My voice too quiet. *Yeah, I do.*

Now the perforated sheet of leaves above me is thinning daily, revealing more and more sky. Geese pass overhead. October: the season of schedules and regularity, but I haven't gone back to Ron Bates and asked for work. I haven't bought a newspaper and scanned the Help Wanted pages with a ballpoint pen either, looking for dishwashing jobs or maintenance crews. I've always worked crap jobs, which means that every year when April rolls around I start to itch like a jackrabbit in a cage; I want to go to the woods, or take a canoe trip or head out on a long drive with Deb and Julie—the kind of time one week a year of paid or unpaid vacation doesn't allow—so come May I tell them what I think: that their factories and sawmills and construction companies are the stink holes of the earth and that they treat their labor like shit, and then I walk out the door and cross the parking lot to my truck and go pick up my wife and daughter and drive us somewhere beautiful—a lake or a field—and feel, for at least a few weeks, free.

Come September, I would always go back to another job.

But not this time.

This time I am living on beer and beef and cans of beans. I am losing money and weight and smelling Maggie in the leaves and in the sheets and in the trees and in the air. At night I lie in bed in the trailer and listen to the coyotes up on the ridge and the deer nibbling the grass outside the door and feel no need to light the kerosene lamp or turn on the twelve-volt radio. I have nothing of hers—no shirt, no ring, no book—but that doesn't seem to make a difference; I don't get bored.

And the coffee is good: strong, bitter on my tongue. My chipped mug says HOME COOKING AWAY FROM HOME and, below it, THE MISS BELLOWS FALLS DINER, the place where Deb worked before she left me this April for the man who is able to keep a steady job, the man with the large house down in Vernon where they don't pay taxes because the nuclear power plant does. Where living is cheap because if the plant goes, they will all die quick as fish out of water. Julie too. Julie: my seventeen-year-old daughter who has stopped meeting me in town for coffee.

Julie: long legs and feverish eyes and a habit of looking anywhere but at her old man.

Your coffee tastes like stove ash and water, Maggie would say, reaching her cup out toward me for more. In the afternoons she'd add a splash of Jim Beam. *For the throat,* she'd whisper. That sly, Scorpio grin.

The first time I saw her was at Rich's cabin, a year or so after he and I had moved up here from Mass. When we were twenty Rich bought thirty acres with a run-down hunting cabin on the south side of Whiskey Mountain. Our older brothers had both returned fucked up from Vietnam, and we wanted out of that life, out of our suburban hometowns. *Back to the land,* Rich'd said, grinning, cruising up the side of the mountain in the green Jeep he drove back then. All he wanted, he said, was a place to hunt, fish, and fuck around. I, as usual, followed him. That was how it had been since we were kids: shoot his guns, ride in the passenger seats of his trucks, drink his beers, admire his girlfriends.

That night: dusk, mist rising off the river, the cabin perched on a slope amidst the trees. By then I was living with Deb in Nelson and Julie was a few months old. We left her sleeping in the car and walked up the path to the house. Rich had a bottle of Jack Daniel's out on the table and four half-pint canning jars. *Fill 'em up,* he said. *Want you to meet someone.*

Maggie stepped out onto the porch. She was young,

tan, barely over five feet, a good-size gap between her two front teeth. It took me a minute to notice her eyes: one blue, one brown. *Spooky,* Deb said later, on the car ride home. We poured ourselves glasses of whiskey, and Rich handed us plates of venison. He went through women like he did boots, but I knew Maggie was something he'd hold on to when he told us the two of them had shot the buck together. *Her hand on the trigger, mine on the barrel. Out of season,* he said, grinning in his infectious way.

Maggie smiled and rubbed her big toe against the pine floor. Deb asked her where she was from, and she told us she was from here, that her family had been loggers, that she had lived on this mountain for a while when she was a kid with her horse-logging grandma Sugar Pial, that she waited tables at the ski area now. We nodded. Looked toward the trees. Ate.

Later, stoned out in the grass under the stars, Rich told stories about the two of us, hunting and fishing when we were kids. He told about the time he'd accidentally shot a fawn, a two-month-old speckled thing, and how the mother had hung around our campsite that whole night, love-sick and crazy, rubbing her head up against trees and pawing the ground. He laughed. *We were fucking scared shitless, right, bud?* he said, looking at me, and I nodded. Rich was quiet then. We were all quiet. Deb fell asleep on the grass, and I watched Maggie in the moonlight and wondered why Rich had told that story; I remembered

what that dead fawn had looked like the next morning—
flies clustered around its eyes—and remembered the
sound of the doe's constant pawing. Maggie leaned back
on her elbows and looked up at the stars and said, *That's
fucking awful,* and I thought then how she looked like she
was of this place, like she was some kind of creature or
tree that had grown here, and wondered how it was Rich
had landed something as spectacular as that.

Another snap in the woods behind me, and I turn,
too quick, my heart electric, but it's just two squirrels,
bandy-legged, chasing each other up a pine. They are
lucky—creatures who fuck and scramble through trees
and die—happy. I toss the rest of the coffee onto the
ground, get up off my chair, and start walking up the hill
through pine needles and dead leaves: Maggie's trail. That
day in June we followed the logging road as far as it went,
and when it dead-ended I followed Maggie, who seemed
to know her way. We followed deer paths through the
grass and ferns, noted where moose had scratched their
antlers against the bark, where bears had lain themselves
down to bed.

Maggie paused in a grove of beeches to catch her breath.
She told me about when she lived with her grandma Sugar
Pial, a half-Abenaki horse logger, up here in a tar paper–
covered shack. *Nothing left of it now,* she said. *Wore bur-
lap bags to school over my shoes in winter.* She laughed.
They called us the Robinson Crusoe kids.

I scraped the bark off a stick with my fingernail. I'd
grown up in the suburbs.

*Not that it was bad. It taught me that the woods is the
best place to be.* She blew at a mosquito that was circling
us. The mosquito disappeared and Maggie dug the toe of
her boot into the ground and looked into the trees. *Hey,
Pete.*

Yeah?

You miss Julie?

I looked at my boots. *Of course.*

Well, go find her.

She walked toward me until she was standing a foot
away, then looked up into my eyes. She wore a sleeveless
cotton top unbuttoned at her neck, and I could see the
soft, gently lined flesh between her breasts. She touched
my chin with her finger, ran it along the line of my jaw,
then turned around and continued walking up the hill,
and I followed her legs and her boots and felt my stomach
go sick with joy and with fear.

Now at the top of the ridge I pause where Maggie and I
stopped: a small clearing of wood ferns turned mustard
from frost, scattered amid boulders. I'm out of breath; the
muscles in my legs burn. I turn around and catch a view
of the top of the mountain. There's a little overhang and
below it a flat spot where Maggie said the whiskey still
once was. *Whiskey in Vermont?* I asked her. *Thought you
were Puritans.*

She raised an eyebrow at me. *I look like one?*

No. I smiled. I was standing so close, I could see beads of sweat on the skin of her arms.

Hey, Pete, she said, looking into the trees.

Yeah?

Hold me?

Sometimes your body condones something before your mind. I reached out and held her and she put her head on my chest and I thought, *Rich's woman, Rich's Maggie,* but I didn't let go. I stroked her hair and breathed in, put my hands on her arms, and wondered what on earth she was after, what the hell she wanted of me. When had I ever made a woman happy? What the hell did I know what to do with her sadness? She smelled like coffee and sweat and the woods we'd been walking through: the sweetness of hemlocks and pines. Then she pulled away without looking into my eyes and continued on up the trail.

It wasn't long after she met Rich that she moved into his cabin. She didn't seem to have any family around anymore, or if she did, I never saw them. She planted a little garden and a few flowers in the small clearing. She seemed, back then, in love with Rich in a way that made Deb and I shy each time we drove home after being with them. It felt like there was something about life we didn't know, or something about each other we didn't dare explore.

Rich threw wild parties at the cabin—coke, whiskey, bonfires—and started his concrete business. Maggie stopped waiting tables and Rich bought her a brand-new Honda. We all hung out still, but Deb said there was something about Maggie that didn't seem right; she said she partied too hard, drank too much. She would crank the music on the stereo in that cabin, let her hair down, and shake madly in her tight stone-washed jeans and plaid shirts. In the mornings she was quiet and shy, a little stiff, like there was somewhere else she wanted to be. She would glance out the window toward the woods, then run her fingers up and down Rich's forearm while he talked, and I used to think, *Damn, Rich, damn.*

Pete, she said that day, here on this ledge where I now stand, her head against my crazy beating chest.

Yeah?

Sleep with me.

Like I said, sometimes the body outthinks the mind. I slept with Maggie that day up here on these ferns, and later in my bed, and later still on a blanket out under the pines.

After that she showed up every day. I never knew what time she would come, only that she would. I stopped going to cafés or bars, just waited out my hours in the trailer reading what books were there—some Robert Parker novels and a guide to wild mushrooms—and making quick trips into town for coffee and beans and ground beef and beer. I lived for that moment she appeared at the edge of my clearing. *Hiya,* she'd call out, grinning, and I'd be out that door ready to go faster than I could say why.

She took me all around this mountain. She knew where the springs were—buried amidst ferns and saplings, water sweeter and colder than anything—and where woodsmen had hidden tin cups a half century ago. She knew where to find the old cellar holes and the stone walls and logging roads that ran between them. She knew the deer trails and the overturned tree roots where bears slept in winter and a small cave on the far side that her grandma Sugar used to say was an Indian hideout. She stared into that cave, her eyes narrowed, as if there were ghosts in there whose voices only she could hear.

Ten years after Maggie moved in with Rich he started building a new house at the bottom of the mountain. It had a grand entryway with marble tiles and twelve panes of glass in the front door. Two years after that Rich made a contract with Ron Bates, who started building houses that popped up like bales of hay in the fields around them, and a year after that he tore down the old hunting cabin.

I like your house, I told Maggie the first time I saw it finished. She stood barefoot at the kitchen counter in cut-off blue jeans and a sweatshirt, balanced like a flamingo with one foot pulled up against her thigh. I had come into the kitchen for a beer; Rich was in the living room watching a game. Maggie poured some Bacardi into a cup of Coke she had perched on the counter.

I think it looks like ass, she said, unsmiling. She looked out the window at the big houses across the field. Rich had started working twelve-hour days and coming home late, and I guessed it was her unhappiness he was trying both to quell and to escape.

It's not so bad, I said, running my hand over the smooth marble of the counter. *I'd take it.*

She chuckled. *Bullshit. No you wouldn't.*

I blushed. She was right. There were some things I thought belonged in fields, and some things I thought did not.

Hey, Pete.

Yeah?

Do you remember the man I married? She glanced toward the living room.

Rich, I said.

Maggie raised her eyebrows at me. *Yeah. Rich. Used to say I was all mountain. That that's why he loved me.* She laughed from deep in her belly. *And the girl I was believed it.*

Maggie preferred to walk the long way, taking our time bushwhacking over ridges and across streams and through the dense swamp pockets of hemlock and pine, getting lost and then somehow touching on a familiar logging trail again and feeling found.

Trees, she said one day, *I love goddamn trees. Just like a goddamn hippie.*

I laughed, shrugged. My uncles and dad worked the big sawmills in Mass, so our lives had hatched at different points along the line of the fate of trees: her people cut them down and hauled them out of the woods, and mine sawed them into planks and loaded them onto big trucks headed south to Connecticut and New Jersey and New York.

Those assholes building the houses down there, she said, gesturing toward Rich's field, where still more houses were being built. *Those assholes don't know their dick from their ass.*

I nodded again, but I wasn't sure I knew much of anything either, when push came to shove. I'd worked for Ron Bates plenty. All I knew was I liked sharing the woods with Maggie. I liked the way she stepped carefully, and stopped to breathe things in, and bent over a track in the mud and named her find. *Coyote,* she would say. Or, *Fisher.*

Sometime in July she told me about the miscarriages: three in five years. She didn't look at me when she said it, just lay in my bed with the sheets around her lower half. She was drinking, and I think if she'd been sober or looked at me, she wouldn't have told me at all, so I was careful not to meet her eyes. I reached for my cigarettes and lit one and thought briefly about one time, maybe five years earlier, when I'd seen her sitting on a stump at the edge of the clearing outside the new house, twirling

her hair in her fingers and staring out into the woods. I
thought of that love-sick doe I'd seen.

I didn't think you wanted to have kids, I said finally.
My voice was all in my head.

Maggie laughed but the laugh meant something else.
She tipped her head back, baring her long neck, her col-
larbone. *Yeah. Me neither. Hey, Pete.*

Yeah?

*You tell Julie about trees? You take her into the woods
with you?*

No, I said, my heart buckling in my knees, some new
kind of pain settling there. *But I should, huh?*

Yeah. Yeah. Fuck yeah you should.

I go right at the end of the logging trail, scramble up the
ledge, skin my palm on some loose rock. I wipe the blood
on my jeans and stop to take a leak. The high-contrast,
warm light of morning has changed to a cooler blaze that
settles on the trees and leaves and makes the oranges and
reds and yellows almost bland. It's my least favorite time of
day, when the hours feel longest, like they will go on forever without the respite of dark or drink. The birds have
quieted and the mist has burned off, and I start down the
west side of the hill, sliding over patches of leaves, swear-
ing, wishing I had something to eat or drink. I half run,
half skid down the steepest section in my tennis shoes,
pushing branches away from my face, hoping I don't fall
on my ass, half hoping I will. Partway down I catch a

glimpse of the trailer's roof: a shock of white amidst all those trees. Something moves there in the clearing next to it, and my heart jumps—*Maggie!* I think first, and then *Rich*. But it moves again, and I see it is just a doe, standing there in the clearing, feeding on woodland grass. It startles and jerks its head, sniffing, then darts back into the woods. The trailer door swings open in the breeze. *Home,* Maggie once stood here and called it, reaching for my hand. *Our heavenly little woodland home.*

Every day she came. Summer grew lush and too hot, and the woods filled with mosquitoes. The dying maples started to turn, and the sumac berries ripened. I never asked her where she told Rich she was going or what excuses she made up after the fact. I didn't know what she was after, and that feeling terrified me, but I wasn't going to risk anything by asking.

In August she started getting careless and I started getting nervous. She'd show up on weekends when I knew Rich was home, or at least when I knew he'd be wondering where she was when he got there. She'd wait until it was almost dark before going back down the logging trail.

You think Rich'll be hungry for dinner? I'd ask.

You think I give a fuck? she'd reply, smiling. She wasn't checking her hair or her face in the mirror before she left; she wasn't bothering to wash under her arms or between her legs. She was also growing fleshy and talkative in a way I'd never seen her. Maggie would lie back on the lawn chair outside the trailer and look up at the stars popping out of the dimming sky, play with the label of her bottle, and talk.

This'll be our life, Pete. You, me, a trailer and a cooler of beer and bear meat and moose skin. You wanna be a trapper? I think you'd make a good trapper. The two of us. Fisher cat, fox, mink. They sell for a good price now.

I laughed, but I was thinking of Rich coming home to the big house down the hill with no lights on and seeing Maggie's Honda there in the driveway, of him sitting at the table in the dark, waiting. I was thinking of what was, or wasn't, growing inside her.

Or one night in late August: *Run away with me. Come to Saskatchewan with me. I've never been to Canada. I'm almost* forty. *Come on. A couple of old farts growing old in the trees.*

But I didn't run away with her. I never took her seriously, never believed that a life with me was what she would choose. Now I think I might have been wrong: that maybe her daytime reveries were the closest she came to saying what she really wanted. But I have no way of knowing for sure, or how things would have turned out— whether we would have made it to Saskatchewan, or if we would still turn each other on trapping fur in the deep north woods for survival. Or if that flicker of light inside her would have survived. Or if any of that would have made her, or me, happy.

All I know is this: in early September, heavy rain fell two nights in a row and she didn't show up the first day, or the next. The morning after that I went down the track and found a note on the windshield of my pickup. The paper was soggy, Rich's handwriting almost illegible. It said Maggie's Honda had been found by the side of I-91 next to the Silver Creek bridge, the driver's door open, that Maggie was nowhere to be found. It said, *Goddamn.* I stood there in the leaves next to my truck and smelled that river and the scent of whatever half-empty bottle I imagined lay on the floor of her car. I heard cars and trucks flying north and south at seventy miles per hour. I pictured Maggie's body leaping off that bridge, tangling in reeds and mud, the trees above waving their branches in the wind. I pictured her with her thumb out by the side of the northbound lane, leaving her house and car and the two of us behind, heading where there are lots more trees to get lost in.

I stumble down the rest of the hill, half running, out of breath. At the trailer I throw the door open, cautious as always, but there is no one. When we were boys, Rich was the better woodsman: quicker, quieter, stronger. I know the weight of his feet falling in leaves, I know the silent slinging motion of his arms as he walks, the way his fingers grip a gun. If he killed me, no one would have to know. Maybe Julie would come looking for me, but the body would be gone by then, dragged somewhere decent like a granite cave or to the edge of a quarry ledge and let go.

I open the cupboard and stuff a few stale crackers into my mouth, crack open two beers and bring them back to my mildewed chair outside, and think of Rich. Sometimes at night I walk the mile and some through the woods to the edge of his field and look at the big house; blue flickering lights of the TV, his Ford in the driveway, but I've never seen him. Or knocked. Or gotten down on my knees and begged. I know I should leave, but I don't. Julie will turn eighteen in a month and has said she doesn't want to see me until I dry out. Which I will do. *Tomorrow,* I say, every night, but today there is just this: this walking, this light, this smelling Maggie in the sheets and on the couch and in the dirt out on the lawn. There is heading into the woods looking for traces—some piece of clothing or note scratched into bark, some sign of what it was she wanted. There is this mountain, full of woodland springs and trampled beds and deer and birds and wood-land paths. And there is hoping, too. Hoping I'll round some bend and there she'll be—sitting on a log grinning, her belly round and flush, those animal eyes. That it was all some magnificent joke: Maggie and her ninety-year-old horse-logging Indian grandma camped out in that cave on the backside of the mountain, living on roots and wild mushrooms, laughing at me when I round the bend.

Ha! Those lips those legs those eyes. Those hands to show I'm loved. Or think I am.

I'm about to get up from my chair and go inside when I hear a branch break in the woods behind me. I turn to look but I am too slow. There is Rich, my old friend, with soft blue eyes and a workingman's face, standing three feet away. He raises his arm as if it is a rifle and points it toward my face. We hold each other's gaze, and it is, for that moment, just like I have imagined—my breath cold and uneven, rising and falling, and I think, *Yes, do it,* calm and clear—and then I think of Julie, and what I have yet to show her, or give her, and my heart buckles and he lowers his arm.

Damn you, Pete, he whispers.

I know, I say, breathing. He has lost ten pounds and his arms look withered; I think of the boy I knew and blush.

And then he comes and sits down on the leaf-pocked ground beside me. He sits slouched over his knees and stares, like I do, aimlessly into the dark shadows of the woods, and I think: *What old boys we have become. What fools. What cruel old friends.* And then our eyes catch something moving in the woods on the hillside above us, and both our heads turn, at the same moment, watching that flickering light, believing in it, wanting it, hoping whatever it is will move again.

5

KARMANN

The year we turned seventeen Annie and I played hooky in a purple rusted '57 Karmann Ghia that used to belong to her brother, Jack. It sat between the back of the barn and a Northern Spy apple tree, facing a slope of cow field and a creek with banks grown up in sumac and pin cherry and wood ferns. Above that creek was a small hill covered in white pine and hardwoods, and above that was sky. Jack had blown the engine six months earlier on Route 100, towed it home with a rope and a Dodge truck, and since then mice had given birth in the stuffing of the seats, leaves had blown in the open windows, and grass had grown up through the hole in the passenger-side floor. She smelled of mildew and mouse and rotting leaves. We didn't care; she was ours. We called her Karmann.

November: the sky steel blue, ashen in places. We smoothed our fingers over the cigarettes we were rolling, tapped our thumbs on the steering wheel, sang the words we could remember of Neil Young's "Helpless." I stuck my cigarette between my lips and breathed in. "Tastes like rat's nest," I said, coughing.

Annie closed her eyes and inhaled. "I like it," she said. "Makes my throat burn."

Jack had left for Vietnam in April, a few weeks after the engine blew, and the Drum came from the bottom of his sock drawer. We could have gone to the IGA in Nelson and bought fresh pouches, but we liked smoking the free stuff we scavenged from Jack's various hiding places best: dresser drawers, backpacks, pockets of his jackets and jeans. Jack was everything this place was not: he picked apples in the fall in order to drive himself around the country every winter; he listened to music no one else did—the Flying Burrito Brothers and Mississippi John Hurt—and had a picture of Grace Slick tacked to his bedroom wall; when he danced he would tilt his head back, close his eyes, and shake his skinny hips. He was the only man I knew who danced.

"Hoo," Annie said, blowing fog onto the windshield. The glass clouded over, then cleared again, showing the heart Jack had scratched with a nail into the hood one night when we were stoned.

"Fucking cold," Annie said. I nodded, feeling the seat's icy cracked leather through the butt of my jeans. We had taken to wearing men's blue jeans and wool jackets we found at the Salvation Army. Annie's jeans had a hole in each knee, and her jacket smelled like pine pitch; mine smelled like the smoke of some World War II veteran's pipe. We were growing our hair straight and long like the women on the back covers of Jack's records and had stopped wearing makeup. It wasn't what boys were into, but we didn't care. We were virgins still. Annie wanted to look like Joan Baez, and sometimes did. She was that beautiful. I wanted to look like Grace Slick. "Why her?" Annie asked me once. "You don't look anything like her."

"No reason," I said, swallowing, thinking of that poster on Jack's wall.

"You look like trash," Annie's mother had said to her one day, glancing up from the pile of laundry she sat folding. Mine had squinted her eyes and said, "Clare, you could be so pretty. And Annie, she used to be so pretty too."

My mom taught second grade and raised me alone. In her free time she made beautiful gardens with neat edges around our white house and was the captain of the bowling team in Nelson. Since Jack left, Annie's mom had stopped cleaning or cooking or leaving the house. She reached two hundred pounds and sat out on the porch crocheting doll-size American flag blankets to give to the American Legion. *Loony as the bird on North Pond,* Annie said. Her dad had gone on with life as usual: rising at dawn to milk their two worn-out cows, going to the lumberyard at six, coming home twelve hours later to milk again. Annie was getting by doing what she and I did: skipping school, smoking what we could scavenge of Jack's tobacco, imagining the places we would go if that car would only drive: Mexico, Arizona, California.

Jack had been all those places. He used to send Annie postcards from the road, which she had taped to the dashboard. One showed a roadrunner crossing a two-lane highway, a saguaro cactus waving in the background, the sky the orange of varnished pine. Another showed a white sand beach in California, grass ablaze with wildflowers, BIG SUR swirled in neon-pink cursive across the top. On the back of the card the names of some of those wildflowers were written: sticky monkeyflower and baby blue eyes. *Baby blue eyes reminds me of you, the prettiest sister in the state of Vermont,* Jack wrote to Annie in handwriting as restless as a ten-year-old boy's. In the last few years when Jack came home for apple season he would take Annie and me places: the quarry in Dorset, the Northfield Drive-In, once, in early December, sledding by moonlight on Whiskey Mountain. On that ice-covered hillside he had put his lips next to my ear and whispered something that sounded like *beautiful,* before flying down that hillside with a blind whoop and holler.

Annie leaned her head back against the leather seat and started picking at the loose stuffing that exploded from the cushions. *"If you're going to San Francisco,"* she sang, then hummed a bit. California was where we wanted to go most: a place our mothers had never been and would never go, a place where we thought no one believed in war.

"Be sure to wear some flowers in your hair," I finished the line.

"California dreaming," Annie said, scratching frost off the window with her fingernail. Earlier that week Mr. Davis, the new history teacher, had shown us photos of people sticking flowers into the barrels of rifles in Washington, DC. "Not everyone believes in war," he had said. Mr. Davis was young and from elsewhere, with sandy blond hair. Most girls were in love with him.

I was in love with Jack. When we were kids he taught us how to light fires without matches, how to do wheelies, how to build forts in the woods by the creek. "Like this," he said once when I was nine, taking my hands and showing me how to bend a sapling and hook it into another to make a frame. I could feel his breath on my cheek, could smell his unwashed clothes. His best friend, Trevor, a big kid with a spongy face who lived in a cabin down near the river, would say, "Dumb girls," when Annie and I were around, but Jack would just shrug and wink at us. "Wildcats," he said with a blue-eyed, innocent grin.

"Fucking winter," Annie said, and started to shiver. She took another drag of the cigarette and coughed.

"We could go back," I said.

"No way," Annie said. "I'm driving this thing to California. That's why we're so cold. We're driving through the plains of Nebraska." Her thin fingers gripped the wheel until her knuckles turned white. Her gray eyes blazed.

"Look at them buffalo," I said.

"Indians," she said.

"Bucking broncos," I said. We weren't smiling.

In December Annie got a letter from Jack. It was midweek, morning. We sat in Karmann watching snow skitter across the frozen fields. No one seemed to care if we skipped school—worse things were happening all over: three kids had crashed and died on their way home from the Five Flies outside of North Bennington; a selectboard member's son had disappeared into Canada; a girl had gotten knocked up and tried to kill herself by drinking a bottle of Lysol. Snow blew in white gusts across the silver grass and drifted toward the frozen-over creek. Annie read the letter out loud.

Jack didn't say much about Vietnam. Instead he told her all the things he missed about home: driving up to Indian Love Call and diving off the deep end into cold black water; the smell of hayfields at night in June; driving across the US of A with its flat, open spaces; going into the woods and feeling safe there. He said he never felt safe where he was. Never. He told Annie to live boldly, to not end up like their parents: ghosts on a farm with a couple of dried-up cows, or like Trevor, stuck in a town that would never change him. He told her when he got back he would take her on a long road trip to somewhere exciting. *Light up your eyes,* he wrote.

Annie folded the letter and stuck it in the back pocket of her jeans. "Jesus," she said. "I wish we had rum."

"At ten A.M.?"

She shrugged. "Why not?"

A nurse from the state had started checking in on Annie's mom; her house was smelling like cat piss and unwashed clothes; she needed diabetic wraps on her legs. Her dad spent more and more time in the barn where he used to milk forty Jerseys when he was a boy, just standing quietly now in the empty stanchions.

Annie looked down at her hands. "You think he'll make it?"

"Who?"

Annie rolled her eyes. "Jack."

The wind had let up, and the field was still except for the snow's settling sheet of white. One of the two cows lumbered around the corner of the barn. It looked our way, then back toward the fence. The ground of the paddock sponged black mud under its feet. "Yes," I said.

"Me too," Annie said, picking at the rip in the knee of her jeans. "But I can't fucking wait. I fucking hate waiting. We're all just fucking waiting."

"Everyone here is waiting," I said.

"Flipping their wigs, waiting," Annie said. It was true: we were all waiting for the people we knew and loved to disappear, or die, or not.

Annie squeezed her knees together tight and grabbed the steering wheel. "You ever want to go somewhere so bad you'll do anything just to get there?"

"No," I said. "I don't think so."

Annie nodded, then reached into her pocket and rolled us each another cigarette. It didn't burn so much going down; our throats were toughened. A gust of wind picked up and blew a piece of stray scrap metal across the yard.

"This place is going to hell," Annie said.

"Aren't we too?"

Annie laughed. It was like a streak of sunlight in that car. "Guess so. Yes. Hell."

A warm January day, snowmelt in the ditches and patches of bare dirt by the side of the road. We walked back toward school, kicking our boots into the blackened snow. Trevor drove by in his Dodge pickup, then pulled onto the gravel edge in front of us. A year ago Trevor and Jack had pinky sworn that if either of their numbers got called, the other would go too, but Trevor's number hadn't been called, and he hadn't enlisted. It was something the whole town knew. Now he had a job at the sawmill and a cabin of his own down by the river. Since Jack left, he kept his big shoulders pitched forward and his eyes on the ground.

He rolled his window down as we got near, sat looking out at the road in front of him.

"Trev," Annie said. I had only seen her talk to Trevor once since Jack left. She had called him a phony bastard and a ball-less wonder.

He glanced at Annie. "Hi," he muttered, blinking, then turned back toward the road.

Annie grabbed the truck's door handle. "Where you going? Anywhere fun?"

He shook his head. "Nope. Back to work. Want a ride?"

"Nah. Hey, Trev," she said, digging her boot into gravel. "Take us somewhere fun sometime. Take us somewhere Jack would have taken us."

Trevor looked at Annie for an instant, then at his hands on the wheel. He picked at the scab on his left hand, and it started to bleed. "There's a party Friday," he said.

Annie nodded. "That'll do."

That afternoon Mr. Davis showed us pictures of blind and burned kids in Hiroshima. He showed us a picture of a baby who had no eyes. "Imagine that," he said, shaking his head. Annie took a jackknife out of her pocket and whittled a peace sign into the plywood top of her desk. Below it she wrote, "Fuck."

The party was down Auger Hole Road at a house with red asphalt shingles and balsam-green trim, tucked into the far end of a field. Old hatchback Saabs and Volkswagen Bugs filled the driveway; a motorcycle perched near the door. Annie tugged at my coat sleeve. "Jack's kind of people," she whispered. "Far out." Ski bums and college dropouts and remnants from the communes near Brattleboro had started moving into places like this in the woods; the selectboard and my mother were worried about it.

Inside, people sat on couches and crammed into the small kitchen. The room smelled like beer and wet dog and pot. Trevor went over to a corner and started talking to a woman I recognized from behind the register at the IGA. I recognized a couple of other people too, people I had seen with Jack at baseball games or the Northfield Drive-In. One wheezed into a Jew's harp; one plucked a banjo. The song appeared to have no tune.

Annie squeezed my hand and went to the gas fridge, where people were getting beers. She pulled two out, handed me one, and nodded toward a guy with blond hair pulled back into a greasy ponytail who I hadn't seen before. He looked about thirty. "Come," Annie said, looping her finger under my belt and pulling me over to where he stood leaning against a door.

"Hi," she said. The guy passed a joint to the friend he was talking to, looked us up and down, grinned.

"Hi," he said. "Who are you?"

"Annie. Jack's sister. This is Clare."

"Oh," the guy said. "Jack. Yeah. I can see him in you." That grin was still smeared across his face. He handed Annie the joint. "Hit?"

"Sure," Annie said. She took a hit, then another. She started nodding her head and moving her shoulders to the music. "Thanks," she said. "That's good."

"Laced," the guy said, winking at Annie and passing the joint to me. I shook my head. He shrugged and told the friend he was talking to that he rode an Indian, said something about spark plugs in winter. Above our heads a clock in the shape of a dog stuck its tongue out and made a licking motion every time the second hand hit 12. Annie watched the guy, sipped her beer, smiled. I didn't want to stand there; I hated the guy with the ponytail. He was nothing like Jack. He was lacking joy.

I went across the room and sat down on a yellow couch near a wood stove that puffed little bursts of smoke. Paintings of wolves and deer looked out from the pine-paneled walls. A guy with a red bandana tied around his head put Otis Redding's "Love Man" on, and two women started dancing. I leaned back against the couch and watched the way they shook their knees and elbows, the way they tossed their heads back and made their bodies loose. I thought of Jack dancing: those shaking skinny hips, his sad, buttery grin, how if he were here, I would get up and dance too. I would shake my small breasts and my big butt. I would close my eyes and wouldn't think a thing.

The last time I'd seen him was in April, a few days after he'd blown Karmann's engine. He stood bent over the open hood with a socket wrench in his hand. He banged at something and swore and kicked a tire of the car. I had come to see Annie, but I stopped there in the driveway behind him. The air was damp; little white snowflakes came down every now and then and melted as soon as they hit the ground.

"Hi," I said.

Jack straightened up and turned. "Clare," he said, smiling a beam of light right at me. "What's up?" It wasn't a question. A woodpecker made a racket on the roof of the barn.

"Here to see Annie." I pulled my jacket up around my ears and squeezed my arms against my chest. I knew he was leaving soon but wasn't sure when.

Jack looked at the woodpecker on the barn and then at the line of trees near the creek and then at Karmann. "She's a goner," he said, nodding toward the car.

I nodded.

He shrugged and glanced up at the tarnished silver sky above us. "Goddamn," he said, quiet, then looked down at his boots and rubbed the toe of his left one into the ground. I thought of that night in that moonlit snow-covered field and the word he might have said: *beautiful*.

Then he looked at me. His voice was little more than a whisper. "It's terrifying, you know?"

"I can imagine," I said. I felt like I might cry, but kept it down there in my throat.

"I never really thought it would be me." The woodpecker made a racket again. "I just never thought."

I nodded and looked at the ground. More flurries came down. One landed on my hand, and in the split second before it melted I could see its crazy symmetrical flower design.

"Hey, Clare, you know something?" I looked up. His eyes were Annie's silver-blue color and wet. I started to shiver and couldn't stop.

"What?"

He smiled. "You're a cool girl. Real cool. I've always thought that."

I felt my cheeks go hot, and then the heat went all the way through my body. It settled in my feet, where it turned cold.

"All right," he said, nodding once, then picked up his wrench again and bent back over the car.

I started for the door. "And so you know," he called out. I turned around. "I'm not gonna die." He grinned then, and I believed him. He couldn't die. I waved once and turned and went through that kitchen door. A few days later he left on a bus from Nelson.

Annie and the ponytailed guy were alone now, passing a bottle of whiskey back and forth. A strand of her dark hair had caught in one of the buttons of his leather vest, and she was trying, halfheartedly, to tug it loose with her fingers. He put his hand on her shirt over her breast, then put the joint between her lips, grinning.

A skinny guy with acne sat down next to me and started talking about farming. He said it was the wave of the future. I nodded and sipped my beer and looked away. The guy in the red bandana put a Led Zeppelin record on, and half a dozen people started dancing. I thought about California—sunshine and ocean and wildflowers and white sand beaches. Not this closed-in dark room that smelled like wood smoke and the damp, mildew odor of wool and sweat.

The room grew louder, blue with smoke and noise. I looked around for Annie but couldn't see her. Another song came on. The guy next to me said farming was the farthest-out thing since the advent of electricity. I looked at my hands. Then the door of the house burst open. Cold air flooded in and a little woman in a parka stood there gasping. "Whoa!" she called out. "Fucked-up girl out there."

A group of us rushed to the door. Out in the dark field people called out *Where?* And *What happened?* And then someone shouted *UFO!* and suddenly everyone was pointing up at the sky saying, *Cool, man,* and sticking out their thumbs like hitchhikers and laughing. I looked up too, but all I saw was a little bit of the Milky Way straight above me. The woman in the parka came toward

HALF WILD

me in the dark and grabbed my arm. She was tiny and the
parka came down past her knees. "Your friend," she said.

I stumbled across the dark field after the woman. In
the grass at the edge of the field a motorcycle had tipped
over and Annie lay sprawled on her back. Her eyes were
closed and the guy with the ponytail was bent over her
saying, "Wake up, wake up," and then, "She's breathing.
She's breathing."

The woman in the parka started crying. "She was just
sitting on it," she said. "And then she closed her eyes and
fell over."

I got down on my knees and brushed Annie's face
with the back of my hand. From behind me I heard the
door of the house slam and felt Trevor next to me. "Oh
fuck," he said, picking her up and carrying her across the
field to his truck. "I'm driving. You hold her, 'kay?" So I
got into the passenger seat and held her.

Her breath was steady and smelled sweet like mari-
juana and whiskey. The stars were sharp and bright, and I
watched them as we drove and all the other things too that
were lit up by the headlights as we passed: rusted train
bridges and tipping silos and vacant barns and the cool
streak of Silver Creek. He and I didn't talk, just cranked
the heat and listened to the sound of the air coming out of
the fan and to the gravel under the wheels and to the motor, and for a moment I thought I might fall asleep there
with Annie in my arms, the hot air on my face, Trevor
next to me, shaking, muttering *Fuck, fuck fuck*, Annie

breathing, and me thinking *Thank God. Thank God.* And also: *Stupid, Annie. Stupid.*

※

March and April were cold that year. Ice storms brought trees down; snow fell into the late part of the month. Annie's mom went to a hospital. Her dad tapped all the sugar maples for the first time in ten years and stayed up till midnight tending the fire and watching steam.

Annie and I didn't talk about that night at the party. She stayed home more, skipped school without me. Mr. Davis moved on to the Korean War, which I didn't care anything about. I got some new records: Neil Young's *Harvest,* Joni Mitchell's *Blue,* and John Lennon's *Plastic Ono Band.* I sat in my room listening to them over and over while filling out college applications. Every time John Lennon's "Love" came on I would close my eyes and breathe deep. There weren't any new letters from Jack. Every now and then Annie and I still missed a class or two together, made our way to Karmann.

Snow had gotten into the car and the driver's-side floor held an inch of standing water. If you weren't careful, your boots got soaked, and if your boots got soaked, your toes froze. Jack's Drum was gone but Annie had new packages of Bali Shag.

She sat in the driver's seat and looked out the window at the field: patches of snow amidst the dead grass, ribbons of orange fencing flapping in the wind. The trees were still gray, leafless netting beyond which the sky turned colors and crows flew. Annie pulled her knees up to her stomach and wrapped her arms around her legs. "I miss him," she said, not looking at me. Her voice was from some far-off place.

I nodded.

She rubbed her hands back and forth on her thighs. "And I'm freezing."

"You want to go inside?"

"No," she said. "I don't want to go to California anymore either."

I was quiet. I started to shiver. "Where do you want to go?"

Annie didn't answer. We finished our cigarettes and threw the butts out the windows. She pulled a bottle of Bacardi out of her pocket and took a sip. Giggled. Handed it to me.

I looked at her a long time. It wasn't yet noon. "Sure," I said, tipping the bottle back and feeling the warmth slide down toward my spine.

"Hey, Annie," I said after a few minutes. I wasn't looking at her but toward the back side of the barn where the rust from the tin roof had streaked down the weathered pine. The air smelled of mud and last fall's rotten leaves.

"Yeah?"

"Where's the rum from?"

Annie licked the edge of a new cigarette, rolled it tight,

stuck it between her lips. She lit a match and inhaled and the tip burned.

"Annie. Who bought the rum?"

She turned toward the window. "Trevor," she said. "Trevor. I'm with Trevor, okay?"

I looked at her, but she just stared at the view and put her cigarette to her lips and breathed in.

"No," I said, quiet.

She flicked her head and looked into my eyes without blinking. "Yes. And guess what else?" She lifted up her flannel shirt and showed me her jeans, which were held closed with a fat safety pin. "I'm going to have a baby."

Later that day Mr. Davis told us in history class that his cousin had been killed in An Loc. He laid his head on his desk and told us to read whatever we wanted to read. I looked at a page on the Korean War over and over without understanding a thing.

***

Jack came back. He didn't die. In early August he got off a bus in Nelson with some other local boys. There was no hero's parade, no trumpets or flags, just parents standing on the concrete sidewalk crying and waving their arms and some antiwar protesters holding peace signs, but they all knew Jack and some of them were crying too. I stood at the edge of the small crowd behind Annie and her dad and Trevor and watched Jack step out into the light. The sun was bright in my face, and I had to squint to see his long legs and broad shoulders coming down the street toward us. I had all sorts of things going through my body; I felt for a moment, standing there in the hot sun, that my life was just beginning.

But when Jack got close he stumbled a little on the pavement and grinned down at the sidewalk; a front tooth was gone. "Jack-o!" someone yelled from behind me, and when Jack looked up I saw his eyes were clouded over. They were darker than I'd ever seen them. They were two dark holes where his eyes should be.

Annie ran out into the street crying and calling his name. She threw her arms around him, but he pushed her away so she was at arm's length, shook his head strangely, and started to laugh. He laughed so hard, he had to bend over. Then he walked to their dad's truck and climbed in. Annie and their dad and Trevor followed. I stood on that sidewalk for a long time.

That night they had a party. There was no music, just twenty people or so standing around the kitchen and living room drinking beers. Jack carried a bottle of Old Crow and kept grabbing the butt of a woman he had gone to high school with named Vicki. Annie sat on the couch next to Trevor playing with the label on her bottle of beer. Trevor held his hand on her leg, stroking her thigh, occasionally touching her growing belly, while she sat there watching Jack and twisting that label into little balls between her fingers.

Late that night, after most people had gone, Jack walked up to me where I stood in the kitchen. It was the first time he seemed to notice me, and he put his face close to mine. "Clare," he said, and I felt a flicker of something in my body. He smelled like Crow and his fingers shook. Through the doorway I saw Annie glance toward us, then look away. Jack put his hand on the plaster behind me and leaned his body into mine. He was all bone and muscle. He put his mouth against my ear. "I want you," he said. There was no sweetness in his voice; it was full of something I'd never seen or heard. That's when I noticed his eyes, wet with tears behind the bloodshot. So I let him have me.

In the hayloft of the barn he pulled off my pants and slipped his own down around his knees. He wrestled my breasts and stuck his tongue into my mouth. "I want to," he said, pushing his soft penis against me. But he couldn't. After a while he stopped moving and was quiet. His tears dripped down my cheeks and pooled inside my ears. Then he stood and wiped his nose and pulled up his pants and slipped down the loft ladder. I lay there for I don't know how long before getting up and climbing down that ladder into the dawn.

I walked out behind the barn and through the damp grass to Karmann. I sat in the driver's seat and looked at those postcards of places Annie and I had still never been that were now mildewed and speckled with fly dust. I looked out the window at the marbled cow field and line of shaggy trees and the brown hill and salmon-colored blushing sky. Something moved and I thought for a moment it was Jack, coming toward me, waving something bright in the sun, but it was just a scrap of torn plastic caught on some weeds at the edge of the field. I got out of the car and walked home. I lay in bed listening to "Helpless" over and over until the sun hit the top of my mother's pines. A week later I got accepted to college in Illinois. Since then I've been all over: Mexico, Canada, California. No place is like I imagined. Love is different too.

6

GOD'S COUNTRY

Cora doesn't know much about her town these days, but she knows her grandson Kevin is one of the ones painting the signs and hanging them up by the side of the roads. She knows because he came and knocked on her door a few months back and asked if he could use the barn— said that he and his buddies had some projects they were working on—and since then she's seen them unloading old pieces of plywood, a few cans of paint, six-packs of beer. They park their jacked-up trucks in her driveway and spend a few hours at a time in there with the lights on, a boom box playing country music she can hear through her closed kitchen windows. When they come out they are grinning, feisty, the way her own boys looked after they'd done something they shouldn't have, like lock a kitten in the washing machine or cut the hair off their sister's dolls: that kind of look. Cora can recognize it even from where she sits at her kitchen window sipping her coffee. Not that she'd tell a soul.

Kevin is a nice boy. In two days he will turn eighteen, and she has decided to tell him, on his birthday, her hope that someday he will take over this farm, what's left of it. She always thought her sons would farm here, but one was killed in Khe Sahn and the other moved as far away as possible with no desire to return, and so she hopes that Kevin will; in summer he mows her lawn once a week, in winter he shovels her path, and every spring he helps her take the storm windows down. His mother, Cora's daughter, Stacey, lives in a mobile home down the road with one man or another, and so Cora has always had a soft spot for Kevin: the towhead, the one she used to invite over after school for fresh bread with butter, the one who called her Grandma Thora until he was ten, before they taught him to say his hard *c*'s. A sweet boy. Which is why she thinks there must be some reason for the signs. Something she doesn't know about. Not that she knows much at all anymore.

That much is clear this morning reading the paper. She's pushed her coffee cup aside and sits at her kitchen table reading the story about the signs and thinking about the blacks she's seen here; she sees them when she goes to the IGA or to the drugstore, and every time a small part wonders why they would want to come to a place like this, a place where they have no roots. None of their own people. Lord knows it's not the jobs.

The article is front-page, the headline in bold. It says they have found two signs, rough plywood with spray paint, nailed to trees along one of the two black-top roads that run through their town. Both have said, GOD'S COUNTRY IS WHITE COUNTRY and have had an undeciphered acronym—NHR—scrawled at the bottom. The last paragraph says there is a police investigation, that if anyone knows anything, they are supposed to call. Good Lord. But she won't call; she hasn't seen a thing, really.

She looks up from the table and out her kitchen window. It's her favorite view: ragged fields stretching down to the valley of Silver Creek, then leaping upward into Round Mountain, raging with October color, and beyond that, blue with distance, the silent hills of New Hampshire. The view she's known her whole life. The hills she calls her own. She can't quite place the feeling she has reading the article; it's a feeling similar to the time she stole her sister's cream-colored blouse when she was sixteen, wore it to a dance, couldn't get the yellow stains out of the armpits, and so threw it out in the trash and never told. It's a feeling close to something else too, something she can't put a finger on, and it comes with a surprising bitter sensation in her mouth that reminds her of the taste of the pins she holds between her lips when sewing. But enough of that. There's too much to do in a day to just sit around worrying about the things you can't name or see.

Cora sips the last bit of her coffee and brings her dishes to the sink. Her new cat, Toby, an orange tom who showed up at her door a week ago, rubs against her shins and purrs. It's been a long time since she's had a cat around; when this one showed up she decided it was time to stop having to put mouse poison in the cellar, stop having to empty the mousetraps from under the kitchen sink. A cat. A companion. She hadn't realized she'd been so lonely.

At lunch she doesn't want to read the letters to the editor, but the page is open on the table in front of her, so she does. One points out the irony that the signs have been nailed onto trees on country roads where no black people live. Another says, "The unwillingness to reveal themselves shows a cowardly ignorance and is emblematic of a deep-rooted racism."

Her husband, Fred, was a racist—she knows that now—only it was the Vietnamese who killed his son and the Italians who worked in the quarries he didn't like; there weren't any black people here then. At least that she knew of. Now when Cora goes to Nelson for her grocery shopping she is surprised how many different-colored people she sees—Chinese and blacks and Mexicans, or people she thinks are Chinese and Mexican, though maybe they're from somewhere else. Whatever the case, they're all there in Nelson, the little mill town by the river, living in the houses where the mill workers used to live, tossing groceries into their carts, the kids begging for this or that, just like any kids. Seeing them makes her confused and somewhat pleased too—she likes to think of them running through the woods at the edge of town, breathing clean air, throwing stones into creeks, growing up in this simple place just like she did. A good place to live, to grow up: God's country. That's what Cora's father always called it, and her whole life she's agreed. Her two-hundred-year-old house sits ten minutes outside of town, invisible to the road, on a hill overlooking a field and the brook where mist settles in the mornings and beyond that, more hills, covered with more trees. The world, she thinks, would be a good place, a better place, if people had all been given childhoods, and places, like hers.

But Kevin must know something she does not. Toby jumps into her lap, raises his hips, and she scratches them: that deep and resonant purr. She has read that petting cats is good for one's heart, and Cora secretly likes to think, every time he sits near her, that her heart is going back in time and getting younger. She's seventy-five and doesn't want to die. Though she isn't sure she wants to live to see her home become something different, either.

In the next letter to the editor a woman writes that the kids putting up those signs are "ignorant, hate-mongering idiots." The words sting Cora like a slap across the face.

Not one of those words fits Kevin, who can get the

lawn mower started each spring, can accurately estimate the number of pounds of lime needed for her fields each year to keep them healthy and green, and has helped her fill out her license renewal form without a glitch. She wonders who these people are, writing the letters, and can't help but picture one of her many neighbors with their new post-and-beam houses that are meant to look old, their brand-new European cars, their golden retrievers. Some of these neighbors have never, after all these years, come by to introduce themselves or say hello to Cora, whose father once owned the land they live on. And *hate-mongering*? She thinks of the small boy who used to show up at her house after school, snot crusted below his nose, pale and runny blue eyes, of the warm, fresh bread she placed in his hand.

Toby stands up and rubs his hip bones into Cora's shin. She feels her heart slowing. But that uneasy feeling returns, and with it, that metallic taste under her tongue. Silk blouses and late nights. One night when she was young, bare feet in wet grass, but—young heart! Stop this bickering, this nagging worry. She will go rake leaves; she will rake all the leaves; she will rake until her body is too tired to do anything else.

That night Cora wakes startled. There is no unusual sound: storm windows rattle against the trim, water hisses through the radiator. Still, her heart's a drum and her eyes won't close. A dream, it must have been. She settles her thin body back into the flannel sheets, wiggles her toes like she does, closes her eyes and tries to drift back to sleep, yet she can't help but feel distracted by the sliver of moonlight that makes its way into the room and across her bedspread through the crack between the curtain and the trim. Moonlight: always enough to keep her up, to threaten her vulnerable sleep. Fred could sleep through anything—sick babies, lightning storms, windstorms, teenage sons in pinhole-in-the-muffler cars, sons MIA in the mountains of Vietnam. But not Cora; she was the one to get up and rock the babies, walk the house checking for broken windows and barns on fire, or just lie there in bed next to his thick and sleeping body and worry about their boys and their girl; the this and the that. She thought when her children moved out sleep would come easier, but it has not; old age has made her sleep less, and need, it seems, hardly any at all.

Toby stands up and comes toward her head, purring, pushing his nose into her face. She tells him to be quiet, closes her eyes—squeezing them tight to shut out that pesky streak of moonlight—but the face that flashes across her mind forces her upright. She leans toward the windows and pulls the curtain wide, breathing hard. What made her think of *him*? She hasn't thought of him in years, or pictured his face. Those dark eyes, those gap teeth. French Canadian, he said he was, and that explained enough: that sun-darkened skin and black hair.

French, her father said. *The Chinese of Vermont.* It was what everyone said back then. But she let him dance with her that night she stole her sister's blouse, cream satin with pearl buttons. The barn dance was called by Glenn Orfee from New Hampshire, with accordion, she remembers, and big bass and piano and fiddle, round and round until that shirt was soaked through, the satin stained, the smell of her all over it.

Good God. What is she doing up in the night, barefoot on the cold wood floor, staring at the moon? That was almost sixty years ago: 1947; she was barely sixteen. But Cora cannot sleep. At five she turns on the light by her bed, dresses, and goes to the kitchen to make coffee. Toby the damn cat: making her heart young.

At eight Cora walks down her driveway to Route 100 to get the paper. It was a cold night, one of the first, and the grass glistens with frost. Leaves are scattered here and there: bloodred soft maple and golden sugar maple and honey-colored oak. She takes the paper out of its mailbox and is relieved to see that the front-page photo is of two children playing in a pile of leaves, a jack-o'-lantern grinning next to them. Just like her own children used to do when they were young; it gives her a little pang to think she has no other grandchildren or great-grandchildren to frolic in leaves like that. She feels the same pang during apple-picking season and sugaring season and on days when it snows. *Where are the children?* she finds herself asking, looking down the hill to where they should be sledding, or tasting sweet sap, and that absence is why she has always had such a soft spot for Kevin. This house is, in some ways, as much his as hers. Her great-grandfather, his great-great-grandfather, built it, stone by stone and board by board, and so she hopes someday Kevin will live in it. She used to slather the butter on his bread and pour him glasses of milk and tell him stories of when there were still cows in the barn: how she and her sister made ice cream every night with the thick cream, how they sprayed milk straight into kittens' mouths from the cows' teats, how before they had neighbors or electricity they walked two and a half miles to get to the one-room schoolhouse, and back at the end of the day, and never complained a bit. Kevin always nodded politely when she told him those things, then reached for more bread and held his empty milk cup toward her. Occasionally she would notice bruises on his arms underneath his shirt sleeves, and those times she fed him more bread, made sure she always had some around in case he came by, tried to keep track of what man Stacey was dating at the time, though she couldn't seem to keep it straight. Cora wondered what a kid, growing up like that, heard at night. Those thin walls. When he turned twelve she offered him money—a few dollars at a time—to come help out around the place, and he came: quiet and sweet and ever helpful.

RACIST "REDNECKS." That is the headline just below the picture of the children playing in the pile of leaves. Cora feels her blood burn, but she feels something else too: ill, thin, not hungry. She thinks for a moment of that face in the night: his bright eyes under the trees outside the barn dance where they stepped to get some air, of the way he leaned against the side of the building and looked at her, then belted out Hank Williams songs—"Move It on Over" and "I Saw the Light"—out of tune and so loud that Cora covered her mouth to keep herself from laughing. But enough; she's too old for this. Cora tucks the newspaper under her arm and walks fast so that her calves burn. At the top of the hill she pauses to take in her world: silvery and glistening and cold and clean. Normally its beauty would bring her a surge of joy, but this morning it all feels strangely off-kilter. She looks at the barn and thinks of going in there—just a quick look—but decides against it. She doesn't need to go sneaking around behind Kevin's back.

Inside she lays the paper on the table and pours herself another cup of coffee. She adds a half spoonful of sugar, something she doesn't normally do—has never done before. The article says the group is assumed to be linked to Confederate flags seen in the back windows of pickup trucks in the school parking lot and some racially charged graffiti on a black student's locker. Cora turns toward the window. *More milk,* he would say, reaching that tin cup up toward her.

The letter to the editor on the next page doesn't help, the one that says the hate crimes (that's what the writer calls them) are being perpetrated by poor, uneducated white trash. That's the term the letter writer uses, "white trash," a term that Cora's own father used once or twice and Fred used often, referring not to themselves, or other farmers, or the people they went to church with, but to the people who lived in the mobile home park at the end of Cora's road, the kind of people who had moved here recently with no roots, the kind of people her people, on this piece of land, were not. But what about Stacey? Is that how Stacey and Kevin are seen: trash? Her father had been a selectman of this town for forty years, an upstanding farmer, a God-fearing Christian, a singer in the Baptist choir. When Stacey needed a place to live the farm seemed the best place: plenty of land left. A good spot for a trailer. But what does that make it, her, them, now?

Cora scrapes her chair backward and clears her breakfast dishes. She needs to get away from this house, these words. It's Tuesday, and on Tuesday she drives into Nelson and does her grocery shopping.

It's a beautiful day, the hillsides lush with color, the sky a radiant blue, and Cora begins to think, driving her Chrysler through what feels as perfect as a photograph, that maybe she has been wrong about Kevin. That paint, those boards, that ruckus in the barn—it must be something different altogether. But that doesn't settle her entirely; she goes around a corner too fast and overcorrects, almost sideswiping a blue mailbox.

At the grocery store as she's reaching for eggs Cora's eyes are drawn to a skinny black woman and her daughter ahead of her in the aisle. She admires the tight, neat braids in the girl's hair: how shiny, nearly iridescent. The color of a bantam rooster's tail. When Cora gets to the checkout line, the woman and the girl pull their cart up at the same time, and Cora can't help but notice the mother's slender, revealed waistline: a belt of beautiful, smooth skin. The mother turns to Cora and smiles. "You've got so little," she says, motioning for Cora to go ahead of her in line. Cora is taken aback by the kindness. If feels so rare these days.

On the ride home she thinks about that waist: Cora certainly never wore pants like that, never let her belly show. But an image of herself in a field at eighteen flashes across her mind—her shirt pulled up above her waist, thin fingers climbing her ribs—and again she goes around a corner too fast and drifts over the yellow line and barely misses a gray sedan coming toward her. *Good God. Pull it together.*

She grips the steering wheel, her arms shaking slightly. When she gets home she puts her groceries away and sits at her window and stares at the calm gray siding of her barn.

That evening Cora sees headlights and hears a truck coming up the driveway: the familiar throaty rumble of diesel. It's Kevin's truck, a GMC he has lovingly repainted red and jacked up on big wheels. She's glad he's here; she wants to see him, to remind herself he's a good boy. She wants some grounding. Cora sets down her glass of wine, throws her husband's old wool coat over her shoulders, and walks outside.

Kevin climbs out of the truck as Cora approaches. "Hi, Grandma," he says, smiling and turning to spit into the dirt of the driveway. He wears a Boston Red Sox cap pulled down low, jeans cinched tight around his waist. A working kid's clothes. Nothing hateful or sloppy or "trashy" about it: just the clothes one would wear to go chainsaw in the woods or move bales of hay or fix a truck.

"Hi, Kevin," she says.

He reaches into the back of his truck, pulls out a couple of empty boxes, and smiles again at Cora—a sweet boy, a shy boy, those blue eyes like her own father's. "Need to clean up the barn a little," he says, nodding at her and ducking his head.

"Oh yes, just do what you have to do. I was just coming out to say hello. You want some dinner?" She looks at the trees, the mist, the blanched-out field.

"Nope. Ate already." Kevin is looking at the barn like he wants to go inside it, but he stays where he is, shifting his feet back and forth, too kind to walk away from an old lady. He looks at her again. "Grandma?" He swishes some chew around in his cheek. "You all right?"

"Yes, I'm all right," Cora says, embarrassed to be seen just staring like that. What is happening to her? "Oh yes, I was just coming out to say hello. You do what you have to do," she says, turning around and going back into the house.

But she watches from the window. Kevin goes into the barn and closes the door behind him. When he comes back out, ten minutes later, his arms are full of boxes. He dumps them into the bed of his truck and climbs in, glancing at the barn and then once toward Cora's house before turning the truck around. She looks away quickly so he won't think she was watching.

That evening is beautiful, the hard maples near the house reaching their peak orange, but for the first time ever they don't feel like her own; they feel as unfamiliar to her as exotic wildlife, as peacocks' tails or the bird of paradise she saw on TV. Just boys being bad, she tells herself. Boys locking kittens in washing machines and messing with sisters' dolls. But she can't stop thinking of the girl in the grocery store, of the little blue plastic gem ring on her finger, of the signs, nailed to those trees, and of him. Him. What is this . . . this unnerving? She washes the dishes and wipes the counters until her body clenches with pain and exhaustion, and then she falls asleep easy, early.

But she wakes again in the night. This time she forgot to close the curtains at all, and that upside-down half moon, like a baby's cradle, is staring at her, shocking her with its gaze. And again, that face: high cheekbones, almond-shaped eyes, and thick, dark hair. *Lawrence.* She hasn't thought of his name in years. *Lawrence.* The syllables slide down her throat into her belly, warble there. French Canadian, he said, and she thought that was all.

She hardly knew him at school; he was a couple years older than her, worked at the quarry, had a younger sister named Mollie in Cora's class who had beautiful, thick, dark hair and wore threadbare, handmade dresses. Cora hadn't thought much about him until the night of Glenn Orfee's dance when he came up to her and quietly held his hand out with a crooked smile on his face and a look in his eye she couldn't name, and she doesn't know why but she said yes, and then—those arms, that endless spinning.

The next week he had walked her home from school, smoking his cigarettes and whistling between the gap in his front teeth, singing those off-key country songs. He said his mother loved the radio, listened to it all day while cleaning other people's houses, and all night when she was home, that her favorites were Ernest Tubb and the Carter Family. He said she worked too hard, and that he was grateful for that music. At the corner of Stark Road, he reached his hand out, and she took it, and they walked like that the back way home, across the Maise hayfield and through the woods, not saying much, Cora rubbing her finger along the lines of his palm. She'd never held a boy's hand before and was surprised at the warmth there.

"The quiet one. Who likes to dance," he said after a while, that crooked smile again across his face, to which she had replied, "Quiet but not simple." And a few weeks had passed like that, traipsing through those springtime woods, stepping over logs and crossing Silver Creek and getting out of breath on the last hill up to the farm, and then his hand slipping from hers and her turning to see him wave and grin and disappear back down the path from which they'd come.

Sweet Jesus, it's too hot in her bedroom. She throws the covers off and lies there on her back in the moonlight in her thin cotton nightgown. Her body has always been slender, small-breasted, not at all like her sister's voluptuous curves, and for years she lay next to Fred and wondered if her body was the kind of body he really wanted, or just the warm flesh that happened to be next to him. Now, lying in the moonlight without the covers, she realizes that after twelve years of living alone she has come to love her thin body, its jutting hip bones and small breasts that have never gotten in her way or weighed her down. Lawrence touched them once. Oh God. For a moment she can't breathe; her skin erupts in goose bumps. Stop this. But she can't. Or won't. It was one of the last days of school, late spring, and they walked up that path toward the farm. Before they reached the open fields, Cora stopped in a clearing of hay-scented ferns and sat down, flattening the cotton of her skirt over her knees. He sat next to her, both of them looking into the trees in front of them. He took his cigarettes from his pocket and lit one, and Cora reached out and asked for it with her fingers, and he gave it to her, smiling as she put it to her lips. Then she lay down in that bed of ferns and closed her eyes and heard a jay's screech above her and then, that speckled light flashing against the dark of her eyelids, felt fingers touching the skin at her waist. Tobacco-scented. Slender and callused. Then she felt those fingers climbing up her skin, up and under her cotton blouse, up and over her ribs, until they landed on her left breast, and stayed there, not moving. Jesus. Cora can feel it now, moonlight and heat and a tingling sensation that ripples down her whole body. What has gotten into her? Toby, that tomcat, and that black woman's waist, and Kevin, and the newspapers, and the barn, all of it too much for her, enough to send her slipping off solid ground. She closes her eyes. *Lawrence Pial.* That was his name. *Lawrence Pial.*

It's still dark—the clock says 3 A.M.—but she can't sleep; she's been up for hours. She switches a light on and goes into the kitchen and makes a pot of coffee. When it's ready she dumps two spoonfuls of sugar in—decadent, wasteful, so unlike her. So sweet it makes her cheeks burn. She sits with the warm cup between her palms and looks out the window at the barn, lit up in that moonlight. Forty Jerseys used to live in there, calve in there, let down their milk two times a day in there. The paint has worn off the siding, and it's a weathered gray now, a few roof slates slipping. The door, she sees, is open, swinging in the wind. Kevin must not have closed it all the way.

She only saw Lawrence a few times after school let out; there was no longer an excuse to go walking through the woods with a near stranger. Once had been at the Nelson General Store. She sat in the passenger seat of her father's truck and watched as he stepped outside into the light, blinking, and lit a cigarette. Long legs, blue jeans, cowboy boots. His mother stepped out after him, a tall woman with a straight back and dark eyes. Cora ducked back into the shadows of the truck, half-wishing he wouldn't see her, but he did. "Hey!" he called out, grinning and walking toward her, but Cora's father was watching from the pump—she could feel those blue eyes burning behind her—and she shook her head at him, said quietly, "Not here." The second time was at Sunset Lake in July. Cora's sister lay on the stretch of pebbly stones in her bathing suit, two or three boys standing near her, skipping stones across the water. Cora sat in her skirt on a flat white rock a ways off, her toes burrowing into cool, wet mud. It was late afternoon and the sun shone on the water, creating a glare she had to squint across, and it took her a while to see that there were a few people farther off, down at the next grassy beach, a place at the edge of the cow field where not many people swam. They were boys, shouting and jumping; she couldn't tell who. One stood waist deep, back and arms and head silhouetted against the sunstruck water. It was a beautiful sight, and Cora felt her body turn strangely light with curiosity, felt a streak of desire shoot from her breasts down to her legs, and then he dipped into the water and disappeared, the surface suddenly still for too long. Cora felt a tremor in her chest: had she imagined it? The water was resplendent, silent, no movement or splash, and she scanned the far bank, and almost called out for help, almost leapt up to go tell the others someone had disappeared out there, when she saw a rippling, then a flash of underwater sun-darkened skin, and then he flung his head up out of the lake inches from her feet: smiling, water spurting from his wet lips, eyes waterlogged and bright. "You coming in?"

A loud bang comes from the direction of the barn, and Cora leaps up. Her legs and knees ache—that coffee too early, that sugar. The wind has picked up, and the open door is swinging wildly, knocking against the pine siding. She doesn't want to go out there, but what else is she going to do? She slips into her rubber boots and wool jacket and grabs a flashlight and goes out into the dark. The night is cool, dry, full of the windblown scent of apples and rotting leaves. She reaches the barn door and grabs onto the iron handle and swings it closed and is about to secure the latch when another gust of wind comes and the door swings open again, out of her grasp, sending her hundred pounds shuffling backward. She stumbles on the uneven ground, catching herself, but in the moment before she does she imagines falling, her bones snapping like kindling. How long would it have been before Kevin came to find her body, covered in frost and fallen leaves? Another gust of wind blows the door farther open, and she glances, for the first time in a long time, into the barn. The windows on the back wall blaze squares of night-sky blue; everything else is shadow. She can just make out the shapes of Fred's old junk, rimmed in moonlight. A bat darts from one rafter to another. She should go back to the house, climb back into the warmth of her covers. But she doesn't.

Instead Cora steps inside the barn and turns on her flashlight. She can see where Kevin and his friends hung out: a few old armchairs set up next to a low table. On that table sits a kerosene lantern, a deck of cards, an overflowing ashtray, and some darts. Some of Fred's things, she sees, are hung on the walls: a rusted Coca-Cola sign, an ugly life-size plastic reindeer, a rusted milk sign. There are posters she has never seen before too: one of a race car spinning around a track and one of a truck, not dissimilar to Kevin's, jacked up on oversize wheels with two blond women in bikinis in the front seats, the skin on their absurd breasts tan and glistening. *Boys.* She lifts her flashlight upward and sees that there are some other things pinned to the wall. She steps closer and is surprised to find that they are black-and-white pictures of her father:

standing next to a prize bull, riding his International across a field, in his World War II uniform. They must have been in some box out here in the barn. The sight of them makes Cora's cheeks swell with a pride she didn't know was still there; her father was a handsome man who believed in hard work and self-reliance and proved the glory of those things and whose only cause for despair was that he had no sons, just two daughters who could not farm, who married men who would not farm. It's nice, she thinks, to have her father in the barn again. It smells like animal still, and like hay, and like the cigarette butts that are scattered across the table.

Something moves against the far wall, and she catches it with her light: a swallow, flitting out of the rafters and making for an open window. She follows it and when it disappears she notices there is something drawn on the beam in front of her with a marker. Some thin lines, loosely sketched. She steps closer, and slowly lowers the beam downward, and sees it is the outline of an animal. A deer. Its body peppered with tiny holes, divots, and on the table, a bowl of darts. Darts. Into the deer's body. That is all.

A gust of wind slams the door closed again, and the whole barn seems to reverberate. She is freezing; she is shivering; she thinks of her body out there in the yard, covered with frost and broken, she thinks of that black girl at the supermarket, her blue ring and perfect braids, she thinks of Fred, hitting their boys with the thin leather of his sweat-stained belt, of the look in those small boys' eyes. Her light is still on those darts on the table, and when her eyes refocus she sees next to them something scratched into the table with a jackknife. Some letters— NHR—and below it the words NIGGER-HATING REDNECKS.

She reads it again, lowers the light to the floor. She can hardly breathe in the cold. Her Kevin. "No," she hears herself say out loud. No. She feels as if she has swallowed a penny. She lowers herself into the green-checkered arm-chair behind her.

That August of 1947, the last time she saw Lawrence, he came to find her. It was a hot, dry evening, the sky luminous and the night breeze sweet with fresh-cut hay, and no one wanted to be indoors but they had finally gone in, Cora and her mother and father and sister, and were just sitting down at the table, her mother carrying meat loaf from the stove, Don Fields and the Pony Boys on the radio, when they saw the Pials' mint-green Plymouth pull into the driveway.

Her father looked at Cora's sister, who shrugged, and then at Cora, who looked back at him, and then he got up and went to the door and opened it. Lawrence stood there in his blue jeans and cowboy boots, his hair combed back. Cora watched her father look him up and down slowly.

"What do you want?" he asked.

"Good evening, sir," Lawrence said, smiling. "I came to see Cora, if that's all right." He looked at Cora then, and she felt her cheeks go hot; she looked at her plate of food for a moment, then back up.

"What for?" her father said.

He was still looking at Cora, that quiet confidence thrust onto his face.

"There's a dance tonight. Glenn Orfee in Nelson," he said, and Cora felt a streak of heat shoot through her body. Those tobacco-scented fingers on her skin, that spinning.

But Cora's father just looked at her, then at the boy in the doorway, and then he tipped his head back and laughed. "With an Indian? You think I'd let my daughter go dancing with an Indian?" And with those words Cora knew what she should have known all along: that was why those dark eyes and that dark hair and those cheekbones. Indian. Abenaki. *The niggers of Vermont,* her father called them.

"Come," her father said, and Lawrence followed him out the door into the darkening yard and Cora stood up and followed too.

"Don't," her sister said, but Cora did.

They walked into the barn—this barn—and Cora followed. They went past the rows of cows, past their slow heat and the soft rhythm of chewing cuds, into the back room. Cora stopped in this room, amidst the cows, and watched through the doorway as her father put his left arm on Lawrence's shoulder and leaned close to him and said through his teeth: "We don't need no Gypsy-Indian blood on this farm," and watched as Lawrence just stood there, not blinking, or flinching, or nodding, but said, quietly, between his teeth, "Asshole," and then watched as her father swung his right knee into the crotch of the man she had let touch her, and as Lawrence fell back against the wall of the barn, and heard the small whimpering that escaped his lips, and then watched as her father strode out the back door and spit into the grass and disappeared. And then came the moment that Cora has not let herself fully remember since—the moment that she looked at him, and he looked at her, and that she turned, and walked out of the barn, without looking back, without saying anything, without feeling remorse, or love, only a strange kind of pity and fear, and she has never known, and still does not know to this day, whether that change in her was because she knew he was Abenaki, or because of the way he had crumpled, without resistance, into the wall of the barn, or because of that strange sound he made as he took the blow. All she knows is that she left, and went back to the table, and ate her mother's meat loaf, quietly.

Cora cannot breathe. She thinks of that peppered outline of the deer's body against the wall, of Lawrence Pial's mother's beautiful, dark face, of the look in his eyes against the back wall of this barn, and cannot breathe. She feels ill: a reeking bitterness in the pit of her stomach. Coffee, pennies, Kevin: sad, bruised-arm boy or no. And this barn, this hillside, this view and mist rising up out of the valley, off the water: is it, was it ever, God's country?

The door swings open and there are footsteps. Cora swats the beam of her flashlight toward the door. Her heart pounds; she's never been closer to believing in ghosts. But it's Kevin. Just her grandson, Kevin, standing there in the doorway, wide-eyed.

"Grandma? What are you doing here?" He walks toward her a few steps, and she's amazed to think she would have been found, after all, if that door had knocked her down at 3 A.M. He would have picked her up, carried her inside. The early hours of his eighteenth birthday. Her dear grandson.

"Oh, I don't know, Kevin. I couldn't sleep. The door was swinging and I went out."

"Right," he says, looking down at his hands, and she realizes he must come here often, in the middle of the night, to get away, to find a safe and quiet place.

"Sit down, Kevin. Sit down here near me. It's so late. Or so early. It's your birthday." And so he does. He sits down and closes his eyes, his knee shaking, and the two of them are silent, his breath rancid with beer, or liquor, or both, watching the night's blue sky through the open windows, and after a few moments she hears Kevin's breath drift into the breath of sleep.

Cora lets her weight settle into the moldy green-checkered chair, the chair where Kevin sat to throw darts and drink beer, and her body feels small, thin, old, brittle, and she thinks this is the way it will go; Kevin is the way it will go, like a giant sheet being removed, revealing some darker, broken, meaner heart, and she closes her eyes, and thinks of Lawrence Pial, of what she has always wished she had done that night, of what she has never let herself imagine: that she had gone to him, and taken his hand, and pulled him up. That they had slipped out of the barn together into that August darkness and heat—crickets, fireflies, stars—that she had lain down in that grass with him, and let him touch her, and touched him, let her imperfect heart explode with his, let there be born, in that night, in that field, the possibility of something different, something beautiful, something new. But she did not. No, she did not. Cora closes her eyes. The barn is all darkness. Just Kevin's slow, uneven breath and the swallow's tail, flickering. *Oh God,* she thinks. She is old. How long until morning?

7

BARRED OWL

I choose the red dress, knee-high black leather cowboy boots, and aqua blue to dust my eyes. The camper is stinking hot and smells of Jimmy's beer, of creek water, and of stained sheets, which I take to my great-aunt Hazel's once a week to wash, but once a week is not enough in August. Not with Jimmy, not with the camper down near Silver Creek, where the sun doesn't shine long enough to keep bread from turning blue, the corners of my books from curling up at the edges, the smells from sticking around. "That?" I said to Hazel four months ago when I came here asking for a place to stay and she pointed at the teal-colored tow-along camper that had been parked behind the barn for seventeen years.

"There's always the chicken coop," she said. She didn't offer to let me live with her, and I didn't want to, even though that's what the social worker had in mind. Two birds with one stone, pretending I didn't know it. But Hazel didn't want me in her house, and I didn't want to be there. I wanted to be where Jimmy and I could screech like barn cats, fuck like bunnies, pop whatever kind of pill we want to. So I took the camper. "Down by the creek," I said—not knowing that the sun wouldn't shine here till eleven, that it would set at four—so my cousin pulled it down here to this little field that borders the water, dragged a two-hundred-foot run of extension cords down from the barn, and here I am now, three months later, calling it home.

I light a cigarette and step outside, sit on the cement-block step and smoke it. I'm waiting for Jimmy to come. Needing Jimmy to come. The sun went down an hour ago, and the fields are turning that hazy blue of evening that I like, the color of smoke. I don't have a license or a car and my cell phone doesn't work here, so when I get dressed up at night I have to sit outside and wait like this for Jimmy to wonder where I am and decide to come pick me up. Sixteen years old and I crashed my mother's Chevy in a ravine and walked out too quick to hide the half-empty bottle of Bacardi on the floor, and so here I am sitting in fields getting a nicotine buzz on with leather on my feet, a red dress running silky down my legs, my face all made up, and no one to see me but fireflies. Or maybe Hazel. I can't see her windows from here, but sometimes I like to think about her up there at the top of the hill, like a fucking ninety-year-old goat, teeth all splayed, hobbling back and forth between the barn and the house. "Hazel," I whisper. "You crazy old horse of a lady. How 'bout coming and getting high with me?" And then I giggle, picturing her smoking a cigarette or cracking open a beer, but I don't mean anything by it, because really I like having her up there, that light streaking across the field late at night, the sound of doors closing, her lawn mower starting up night and day. "Fucking ghost-woman," Jimmy calls her, rifling through her bathroom cabinets and stashing bottles in his pockets, and I laugh, and then he pulls me toward him onto her bed, and then we are back in that place, that heat and sweet pain and necessity, and oh my God I'm not thinking of Hazel then.

But I don't mind thinking of her now, smoking my Marlboro. That's the name of a college town nearby, full of rich kids—Marlboro—which is the reason I've always smoked them: "Spelled like the cigarette," I'll say, grinning, because I like to think how I'm sitting out in a field smoking a cigarette but I'm also, in some abstract way that turns me on, smoking this place, the whole fucking mess of it: the rich assholes and the punk kids like me and the sad old ladies like Hazel and the do-gooder hippies turned into yuppies or stoners and the ones with second homes and ski chalets meant to look like *The Sound of Music* Swiss crap. Now when people ask where I'm from I say, "Vicksburg, like the song," and giggle, though most people don't know the song. Yeah, that's my hometown. Six generations, baby. Crazy fucked-up place the Japanese and southern bus tourists think is pretty. "Leaves!" they cry out, their buses getting stuck on back roads, falling into ditches and making detours to find the second homes of movie stars. Whoopi Goldberg has a house near here. For real. And once a Japanese woman fell into a beaver pond trying to get a picture of a maple tree reflecting on water. Fuck yeah! I giggle, thinking of them dragging her up out of the water, pond muck and rotting leaves and algae dripping from her face and hair. "So pretty!" I giggle again. Jimmy, who was on the volunteer fire department at the time, said the woman was fine, "just cold as a witch's tits."

There's still no sign of headlights coming down the river road toward me, so I get up and start walking. My cell only works once I hit the pavement, about a mile away, so I can't even call Jimmy. He told me he'd be here by four and now it's eight, and so I hope he's at one of his buddy's apartments: Duke of Hazzard and Skinny Lenny, that's what Jimmy calls them, to their faces and behind their backs. They love it—grin their pocked faces and slap him five and say "Shit yeah" and know that Jimmy will be back tomorrow with however many OxyContin they want. That's the kind of guy he is: the man. My man. Twenty-four-year-old Jimmy with a brand-new Jeep SUV and that beautiful win-you-over shit-eating grin, throwing fives down the front of my dress when we're at parties, saying, "Shake it, Vale, come on, show me what you've got, shake it." And just like a stripper I do.

The river road that winds along this side of the field isn't a real road, it's just a dirt track packed from farm trucks and tractors, so the heels of my boots sink down into mud. I stumble but the grass is worn enough so I can see where I'm going. Just a skinny moon—Skinny Lenny moon—coming up behind Hazel's hill, turning my dress all shiny crimson. I didn't grow up in fields like this; I grew up in Nelson, and it was only once a month or so that my mom would drop me off out here to throw hay bales up onto a truck with my cousin Danny or make strawberry jam in June with Hazel. My mom would never stick around. "It's like hillbilly central out there," she'd say, flicking her cigarette out the window, as if this wasn't where she'd been fucking born and grown up and lost her virginity, no doubt, in some field like this one, but I didn't say anything. I didn't mind it then, getting away from her and her shit. I don't even mind it now, for the summer: this trippy field down by the water and crazy Hazel on her tractor (how many girls have tractor-driving great-aunts?) and the camper all my own where I've hung a picture of me as a baby and a picture of me and Jimmy last summer, swimming, and my collection of miniature owls. Owls—I don't know why, except that I found a couple at a flea market once and they've been popping up ever since—salt and pepper shaker owls, plastic owls, wooden hand-carved owls. I go into the junk stores in town every now and then and look around and buy another for a dollar or two, and so they're lined up on the bookshelf, staring at me when I'm trying to sleep, and the crazy thing is that there's a *real* owl down here by the river that almost every night makes his crazy hooting love song, and when I hear it I turn to my little owls and say, "Hear that? The real thing, you little bug-eyed babies. The real thing."

At the pavement I stop to catch my breath, pull my cell out of my bag. Where I don't want him to be is at a party, without me. Where I don't want him to be is near any other girl. I get two bars on my cell and call Jimmy. It rings three times, and then he's there: "Vale."

"Dude," I say. "It's eight thirty."

I can tell he's at a party by the music in the background. He laughs and yells, "Get your hand off my butt!" And then, "Sorry, Vale. What'd you say? Girl, where you be at?" And when I tell him I'm standing by the edge of the road at the edge of a fucking farm looking hot as melted butter he laughs and says, "I'll be right there."

I can hear his Jeep before I see the headlights—he's pinholed the muffler so it sounds like a pack of Harleys.

"Woman," he says when I open the door. "You look like a goddamn whore out here." He grabs my thigh and I give him the finger and lean over and kiss him on his mouth. He tastes like beer and the taste goes all the way down through my body. I want him to live here with me, though I haven't told him that. He says the woods are some spooky fucked-up shit. He spins the car around at a wide place in the road, but still we go down into the ditch and then peel out, leaving skid marks on the road and mud on our hubcaps, and I laugh and then we're back out on the highway.

The party's at Liz Stokes's house, a dude ranch in a field with three horses and two Beemers and a pool. The doors and windows are open, and JT blasts from the thousand-dollar stereo. Jimmy hops out and grabs my hand, and I leap out the driver's door behind him. Inside there's a fishbowl of pills and everyone I know is there. Jimmy pulls something out of the bowl for each of us and hands me a beer, and I start to shake my booty to JT's beat. My best friend, April, comes up behind me, and we grind together and I whisper, "Sexy ladies" into her ear, and for a minute—I have no fucking idea why—I think of Hazel up at the top of that hill in her house alone and wonder what she'd think if she saw me here, if she's ever heard this music, if she's ever even moved her body the way I'm shaking mine now, say while trying to get shit off a shovel. The thought makes me snort, and I finish my beer and look around for Jimmy but he's gone, so I go to the keg for another. He's probably outside selling whatever pills he's got and I think of the way money rolls through his hands and I imagine the kind of ring or car he might buy me someday and I close my eyes and shake, shake, shake, until I feel hands on my hips and my back— big hands, strong hands, Jimmy's hands—and those hands are around my flat stomach now and his tongue is in my ear and I'm still shaking my hips to the music, still tossing my head, and he is whispering, "I want you," into my ear, and then everything is *all right*.

At midnight people start taking their clothes off and leaping into Liz Stokes's pool. "Come," Jimmy says, pulling me into the master bedroom. He puts two pills on my tongue. My head goes blitzo. He slips my dress down off my shoulders, reaches in his pocket, and pulls out a handful of pretzels. Pretzels—I start to giggle. Through the open windows come the sounds of splashing, of bodies cascading into water, of dudes and girls and every once in a while the whinny of a horse. Jimmy pushes me down onto my back on the bed. He is whispering to me—"Vale, Vale, Valley Vale." He takes a pretzel from the bed and slips it between my lips. "Eat this," he's whispering, and I let the pretzel slide into my mouth and the salt explodes all along my tongue and gums and seeps into the roof of my mouth like some crazy constellation of bright stars. A pretzel! And then Jimmy is slipping my underwear down off my legs and his lips are on my stomach and brushing against my thighs and the sounds of squeals and screams and water splashing drifts in through the open window, and then he is going down on me and someone screams at the pool and oh my God I am no longer in my body I am no longer even a body I am a flame, a globe of trembling light and I am about to disintegrate into that flame and into ash when the lights flick on and Liz is standing in the doorway, stone-eyed, saying, "My mom's home," and

Jimmy starts to laugh so hard that blood comes out of his nose and drips onto my leg and Liz rolls her eyes and leaves the room and I yell, "Fuck!" and scramble to get my dress back on.

He drives me home, popping PBRs and throwing the empties out the open windows. He's laughing the whole time, but he's not looking at me, and my body is some bruised color, so tender I think my skin might break if it is touched. But it doesn't. Jimmy is drunk by the time we get home, and our sex is Jimmy's drunk and stoned sex: fine. Okay. Quick and painless and easy, and I lie in bed afterward with my head spinning listening to Jimmy snore and think of Hazel up there in her house alone in the dark and wonder if she was ever in love, and if so, if this is what came of it, or not.

When I wake up, the clock next to my head says four; the moon's gone, there's a faint rim of blue at the edge of the sky. I reach my arm across the bed, but there's just a pocket of cold sheets. My head throbs and that bruised feeling slides up from my toes back into my whole body and fills it, and then I hear the owl—*Who-cooks-for-you?*—a barred owl. I look up at my little owls on the shelf that I can just barely make out in the moonlight. "Hear that?" I say. The barred calls again and its sound slips down and settles between my legs. I wonder if Hazel hears it, up there on the hill, Hazel who once told me that owls are a sign of the death of something old and the start of something new. It calls again, only this time it's right outside my window on a low-hanging branch, so close I could touch it if there weren't a screen between us. "What the fuck?" I whisper to that bird who's staring back at me, and I think for a moment I might cry, like a fucking baby, but I don't. Its eyes are black, unblinking. They don't look away. They take it all in: me, the creek, the camper, sky. They swallow us whole, and inside its body is stillness: blue velvet, peppered with holes. "What the fuck?" I ask again, to which it blinks its black eyes and flies away, not telling me a thing.

8

WHERE FIELDS TRY TO LIE

It's April, and the kitchen where I sit, sipping a cup of black coffee and watching the light on Round Mountain, has yet to warm from the sun or from the log I put in the cookstove two hours ago, so I get up and throw another log on and open the damper. The wet wood hisses—it will not burst into flame—and I stand there for a moment with my hands searching the matte black surface for warmth, and then go back to the table, and to my still-warm coffee, to stare at the view and watch the sun come.

It's my first morning here: rising in the cold house at five because I can't sleep, stepping outside the kitchen door to take a leak—the remains of last night's liquor streaming through my yellow piss—heating water for coffee and drinking it black at this table where the names of my siblings and me are carved into the southeast corner leg with the dull blade of a child-size jackknife. I was the one who did the carving, as I was the one who did most things, being oldest, and least daunted. Which seems funny to me now, considering how my surviving siblings' lives have been freer than mine, less constricted, less haunted by this place, and that summer some twenty years ago.

This place: a rugged hillside farm with a view of New Hampshire to the east and Round Mountain to the south, built on ledges of granite with red-dirt rivers that look like veins digging trenches where fields try to lie. The buildings: a two-hundred-year-old Cape with peeling white paint, a gray barn, and three smaller barns, each at various degrees of communion with earth. No one has slept in the house since my father killed himself three years ago. When I arrived last night at dusk I found the counters covered in mouse shit, the kitchen door, not latched properly and never locked, blown open in the wind. Which is maybe why this place has seemed so inhabited by ghosts this time around: my sisters in their thin dresses running barefoot up cold stairs; our father's dark eyes glistening toward the television; my mother's bent shoulders and eyes stretched as far as she can see out the window toward the horizon; and my brother—most of all my little brother—with his thin bones and hooded eyes and habit of always turning away.

But enough. It's too early.

I get up and look out the window at the barns and fields that now belong to me. What on earth will I do with them? Because my sisters have chosen to marry men who live eight hundred miles away, and because I'm the one who can afford to pay the taxes and the farmer next door to mow the fields once a year, they are now mine. I thought I had hired the farmer's daughter as well—sixteen, red hair, the spitting image of her mother at that age—to check on the house now and then, to look for broken windows or squatters, but clearly she hasn't been by since the door blew open last. Nor has she swept out the leaves and debris or chased out the squirrels. So be it. I didn't call to warn them I was on my way. I called no one. I'm still not sure I knew where I was going when I loaded my books and clothes into my car while Helen was still sleeping, those books and clothes that still smell like her hair and paints and will continue to for as long as I keep them closed up in bags in the backseat of the car, untouched by fresh air. A six-hour drive and I was here by five. The note she was expecting left on the pillow in my crooked hand with its one vapid word: *Sorry*.

But enough of this: more coffee. Outside two robins land in the damp earth of the yard, then chase each other into the maple tree with the clatter of their sexed calls. The light hits the gray wood of the barn, washing it clean. Home—a facet of my life as substantial as love has been, or work. The place I am always trying to leave or return to, the place that will not let me be. I told that to Helen when we were twenty-nine and first in love; she nodded and looked at me with those dark, serene eyes, full of tenderness and incomprehension. Not everyone feels this way about the place they were born. Not my colleagues, or Helen, whose paintings revel in the beauty of surfaces: concrete, lace, fences. And I envy her, and them, that freedom, and yet wonder who I would be, and what I would think about the world, were I not from here. And then I wonder if such a freedom would make me more jovial, more lighthearted, more lovable, more capable of love.

But who the fuck cares; I look out at the two hapless robins, trying to fuck, and think that even so I would choose this sweet yearning, just as I would have chosen to love, even if that love would lead, as it has, to pain. And it is when I am thinking like this—most often when I'm far away, and more than a few drinks into some bottle of Argentinian Malbec or expensive bourbon—that I become victim to the lies of nostalgia, that they seep into my bones and shade my memories of this place a soft, muted, and lovely gray.

But not this morning. This morning this room smells of cellar dampness and mouse shit, and the driveway, visible through the window, my two-year-old red Volvo incongruent in its center, is a line of black mud leading toward the doorway of the large barn where my father took his life one morning at dawn. So I am not back with any romantic dream of returning to the land. That dream, with all its sweetness, is for others with far more innocence than I will ever know. "I will arise and go now," Yeats wrote when he was still young and in love.

A knock at the door and I jump. It's early—my watch says a few minutes shy of eight. I run my hand through my thinning hair and stand up, bumping the table and spilling a bit of coffee. Standing at the door is the tall, red-haired girl from down the road whose name I have forgotten, the one who looks just like her mother, Jane, Jane who I once kissed—sweet must of hay—behind a barn when we were no more than fifteen.

"Morning," I say.

The girl stands sullenly with her legs spread, her hands on her hips. She wears tight blue jeans, a wool farm jacket, barn boots.

"Hey," she says, her voice muted and flat. "My mom told me to come and see if you need anything. Make sure the house is okay." I look again at my watch and wonder what time she got up this morning.

"Oh, right," I mutter. "Everything looks fine. Just a few mice and squirrels. Thank you."

"Okay," she says, and shrugs, and turns to go, and I realize then that I haven't paid her for watching the house, if that's what it could be called, and that's probably the real reason she's here in my doorway at this early hour.

"Wait," I say, and the girl turns. "I owe you money. Come in?"

She shrugs, peers through the doorway into the kitchen, and follows me inside. I search for my checkbook among the things I've scattered on the counter: catalogs, bills, an English Department newsletter. The girl leans against the fridge and inspects her fingernails, and Helen's fingers flash across my mind: paint-filled nails, long, graceful bones. I find the checkbook and open it and then have to look up at this girl—my mind is blank. "I'm sorry. I forget your name."

"Rachel."

"Oh. Right. Rachel Cole?"

"No. That was my mom's name. Rachel Clement."

"Right," I say. And then, again embarrassed, I realize I don't recall what I said I'd pay her. She is looking over the things scattered across the worn Formica; her eyes settle on the half-empty bottle of Maker's Mark. "Just stuff," I say. An apple blush appears for an instant in her cheeks, and she looks back at her fingernails. "I'm afraid I've forgotten how much," I say.

"Fifty."

"Oh. Right," I say, and write her a check for seventy-five.

She looks me in the eye for the first time, and I'm surprised to see how curious and bright her eyes are—not completely un-innocent yet—and then she is turning and calling out "thanks" over her shoulder, and then she is gone, the house quiet again, and uninhabited, except by

me, and the squirrels, and the ghosts, which are sure to
come creeping back shortly.

My brother Ross was youngest. Two years after me came
my sister Adelaide, a year after her, Dell, and four years
after that, Ross. By the time he was born my mother's
black hair was streaked with gray; her narrow shoulders
had already begun to curve inward. The day she came
back from the hospital with Ross I stood in the yard and
watched my father come out from the barn, a shit-coated
shovel in his hand, and shout, "What is it?" And when my
mother said, "Boy," I watched my father drop the shovel
and go to her and whisk her up into his arms and swing
her around in a circle there in the dirt of the driveway. He
called out, "Nice work, little lady!" and a look of pain
streaked across my mother's face, and then my mother's
mother, Memé, who was climbing out of the passenger's
seat of the car, a small bundle in her arms, shouted, "Put
her down, Jake," and my father set my mother down and
nodded toward the small bundle in Memé's arms. "A boy,"
he said. "Good. Someone else to do some work around
here," and then he glanced toward me, and nodded at my
mother's father, who was getting out of the car from the
driver's seat, and went back into the barn.

I pour myself another cup of coffee and go back to the
table where I can see that barn again, the shifting light revealing weathered pine, streaks of black rot, woodpecker

holes. I can remember the smell of the yard that day, the sweet rotting scent of late summer. I was eight, and I followed my mother and grandmother and sisters, who had appeared from the garden, into the house. I was afraid of my mother's body, of the way she limped and of the smell of medicine and blood that was still on her, and I watched as she sat down on the couch in the parlor and my grandmother put the bundle on my mother's lap and folded the white blanket away to reveal my brother's face. It was a beautiful face—my mother's dark features and straight nose and thin, delicate lips. And then I noticed that his legs were curved in an odd way, and that his left foot—she had pulled the blanket down farther now—was thin and twisted in a way that made me turn away.

"What's wrong with him?" I asked.

My mother looked at me with tired eyes, and her upper lip trembled once. "His legs are crippled," she said.

And I remember then a shiver of disgust and fear and deep protectiveness going through my body, for what would a boy be, here in the world I knew, the world he was being brought into, with legs like that? And what would my father say when he found out? And what on earth would my brother be, when he was old enough to go to school, but a cripple, and later on, when he became a man, but a cripple still? And so I left that room and that house and went down across the fields, high with August grass, to the river, where I sat for a while and tried to calm the tingling in my fingers and my toes and the ice-cold breath that rose like a fountain up and out of my chest, and when I could not I slammed my fist into the earth again and again.

"What are you afraid of?" Helen asked so many times that it stopped being a question and became a plea, on her part, for a man who was not afraid of what she had to offer, of the deep water that love could be. Afraid of oceans, afraid of dinner parties, afraid of barns and their sparrows, afraid of making love without the safety of the dark, afraid of Helen, with her long fingers, attempting to find me in there. "Nothing," I said, every time.

"This won't do," Helen said not more than two weeks ago. "This kind of love."

On the other side of this glass the world is waking: mist rising out of the valley, steam rising off the roof of the Cole and Clement barn down the road. I step back from the window and open it, and the chirping robins assault me with their unbearable optimism. *Shut the fuck up,* I want to whisper to them. Beg them. *Please. Please. Shut the fuck up.* But they do not.

The sun has now reached the top of Round Mountain, and as it crests the highest pines the table turns honey-colored in the light. I feel the warmth on my hands and spread my fingers so the heat can work its way into the creases of my knuckles. Soft and pale, my hands look nothing like my father's—cracked and arthritic—at this age. Fifty: the age when men realize they are growing old and have made little of their lives. My father made it past that—this—ripe age, by drowning himself slowly with cans of Budweiser and hard work and the misery he chose instead of love.

My brother, Ross—hands long and thin like our mother's—will never see five decades, and I am glad, in the only way a surviving brother can be, that he will not have to face this crossroad of manhood. In my most optimistic moments I imagine that he has been set free from it all. But then again some people find that freedom in other ways—without drinking themselves into oblivion, or dying, or so I have been told.

I get up to make myself something to eat. There is a pathetic collection of food on the counter: a loaf of white bread, a bag of Chessmen cookies, a jar of peanut butter: all dull-colored food. Who would have thought I would marry a woman who liked all things the color of blood? Beets, wine, vermilion. A woman who paints skies desert red and fields chartreuse. I could get in my car and drive to the IGA, or better yet, the Stonewall, a place where I am sure to see faces I have not seen in twenty years, aged like my own. But I'm not ready for that. My car would stand out too much amidst the pickup trucks and mud-splattered station wagons, and the color of the food would be no better. I look out the window at the barn and the deep-rutted driveway and at the fields, which are still last year's brown, and farther yet down the road to the peak of the Cole and Clement house, where Jane and Rachel and Jane's husband live, and at the shadow of her father's double-wide next door. If it were a different time, and maybe even a different place, I would put on a wool coat and walk out my door to their place and ask if they have any extra eggs. Just one or two would do. And perhaps some butter. But I won't. Instead I stuff three Chessmen into my mouth and swallow. The sugar pools amidst the remaining liquor in the bottom of my stomach, and I think for a moment I may vomit, but I don't. I just stand there leaning over the counter with my head bowed, thinking how I should buy a sponge and wipe these counters, thinking how I should find a broom, a rag, a cloth of any kind.

My brother learned to walk, eventually, with a crutch and a cane, but he never learned how to clean a stall or drive a tractor. My brother's heart was weak also—that's what we called it, *a weak heart,* and I knew no other medical details. My father, in turn, never learned to love my brother. My father who supposedly, once upon a time, courted my mother with wild roses, and sang, though I never heard them, French love songs. But by the time Ross came along, that sweetness was gone. My father was disgusted by him, as people sometimes are by those whose bodies reflect their own human weakness. He used a pronoun, never a name, to refer to Ross. "You're not bringing *him,* are you?" Or, "What's *he* doing?" Ross, who learned quickly how to make up for his weaknesses by making the people around him laugh. He made spot-on impressions and told absurd and crass jokes and learned to do cartwheels and land on his stronger leg. He had a sweet streak none of the rest of us had. He would limp across the yard, bringing me and my sisters and our mother fistfuls of daffodils and baskets of wild blackberries. He liked giving gifts, and he liked making other people happy, most of all my mother and me.

I open the bag of white bread and slather a slice with peanut butter. I chew and swallow and then do the same with another. "You eat food like it's a chore," Helen said not long ago. "Don't you ever enjoy it?" And I did enjoy Helen's food: wine, oysters, warm, thyme-scented stews. "You eat the same way you make love," she said, her brown eyes laced with tears, and in the moments when I think I may still be lovable, still capable of love, not yet ruined by my father's unloving, that line rings in my ears and in an instant I am back on this farm, no matter where I am.

I down the rest of my coffee, throw my shoes and coat on. I need to leave this kitchen. I stand in the open doorway and breathe. The air is warm against my face, and I let sunlight soak into my aging skin. Spring is everywhere—rotting manure, mud, dirt, pollen, the sugary smell of sap running through trees. I pick up a rock and toss it into the air. It hits the grass with a *pock* and settles back into the earth. I could go inside and start drinking; I could get in my car and leave here; I could go into that barn and light a match to a corner of old hay; I could call Helen—no, I cannot do that. I look at the driveway and think of that summer, of the yellow dust that settled everywhere, of the way it streaked across stones and dirt and wood every time it rained, so much so that my mother said, "Strange, so strange."

I was nineteen, Ross was twelve, and I was already leaving, though I didn't know it at the time. I wanted nothing to do with this farm, or anyone on it. Unlike half my friends—Jack, Danny, Clem—my draft number hadn't been called, so I hired myself out to work at the slate quarry in Jacksonville. By doing so I passed up not only the war but working on the farm like a good son. To add insult to that particular injury, I had done well in school and so instead of working with stone, where my father could at least respect my hard muscles and long days, I was put to work in the office helping with the books. I added numbers while my friends died in jungles and swamps and my father toiled alone in these fields.

I got paid well that summer. Half of it I gave to my mother, who stored the cash in a tobacco tin in her underwear drawer, but the other half was my own, and I spent it on things my father thought frivolous and sickening. I bought leather dress shoes and Levi jeans and, worst of all, a secondhand Volkswagen Bug that my father was ashamed to see parked in his yard. I dated a girl whose parents owned a summer home, a girl who went braless and whose brown hair smelled always like oranges, a girl who was on her way to Wellesley College. By that fall I had secretly applied to the University of Vermont. I thought the world was mine for the taking; I thought at that young age that the self could exist where the body resides.

That summer Ross hit puberty. His cheeks and mouth became fringed with mouse-soft hair, and he started having wet dreams, and my mother, whose hair had turned a solid silver-white by then, took me aside one day on the porch and in a quiet and steady voice said, "Do for him what I can't and your father won't."

So for a few weeks I tried. I helped my brother shave and took the sheets off his bed and washed them in the new General Electric washer we had recently installed on the back porch. One afternoon in early June I invited him up to a deer perch in the woods and we walked up there slowly, him stepping over rocks and logs with great effort and determination, to that spot at the top of the field with a view to New Hampshire, where I handed him his first beer. It was a hot day and he drank it silently and with relish. We were both quiet, simply sitting there in the hot afternoon sun taking gulps of the cold beer, sweat running down the backs of our legs, our eyes looking down on our haphazard farm, littered with broken machinery and little rectangular barns, and out over Round Mountain to Whiskey beyond.

Eventually I asked him about school.

"It's awful," my brother said, then turned away toward the view. I knew he was an outcast in school, and I knew he had lost the older brother who had once been the only friend he needed. It had changed him. He no longer made a fool of himself in order to make us laugh. His body became both a thing to hide and a place for hiding.

"It'll get better," I told him, unsure, and my brother nodded and I opened us each a second beer, which he accepted with a nod, and we listened to the motors and birds that resonated up there on the mountain.

The beer made us sleepy, so we leaned our heads back on the stand and lay there for a while in the sun with our eyes closed, listening to our father's Farmall down below, and to a wood thrush, and to a blue jay's racket, and to a two-stroke engine farther off back in the woods, and I looked over at one point and saw my brother smiling, his face radiating a sleepy, half-drunk peace, and I will always remember that afternoon for the subtle brotherly sweetness that was there, and I will always regret that it was just that one time, and that the rest of the summer I was too busy making cash and fucking a rich girl to ask my brother up to that spot in the trees for a beer again.

The sun is bright now, lighting the whole yard. From where I stand I can hear Jane's farm down the road—the low groans of cows, the clank of a metal gate swinging closed, a tractor engine starting up. I think about who I would be if I had taken over this farm, as I was expected to do, about how regular and comforting the mornings of my life would be—the clock of milk-full udders keeping me from the ponderous fits of melancholy that mornings so often send me into—and right now, for this one moment in the sunlight, I long to hear a cow's desperate bellow from this barn before me so that I have somewhere I must be, something I must do. But there is no one who needs me, no cow or child or woman waking up and turning over in search of the tender release of touch. *Forgive me, Helen.* I sit down on the porch steps with my elbows on my knees, my face in my hands. I breathe in the scent of mud, that dank and harrowing smell that wants, every year, and with such determination, to break things open.

It was not a good summer for farming. Milk prices were in the dirt, and our first cutting had been rained on and lay in the barn starting to mold. The fields were ready for a second cutting, but it rained through the rest of July, and when, in early August, the radio predicted a possible dry day or two, my father decided to risk it. On the fifteenth of August he cut the hay, and two days later he came in from the barn, past these very steps, stood in this doorway, and looked at my mother and me eating breakfast.

"Need your help today," he said, nodding toward me.

"Can't," I said, not looking at him, shoveling a forkful of my mother's eggs into my mouth.

"Need your help. Got to get the hay in."

"I can't," I said again. "I have a job."

My father stood still and looked out the window. He cleared his throat and then said under his breath, "No-good goddamn pansy job."

My mother went to the stove and laid a cast-iron pan down hard.

"At least I make money," I said.

I saw my father's left hand start to shake. That hand had smacked me across the face many times before, but I knew we were beyond that now. "Goddamn spoiled son of a bitch," he said quietly, to which I shrugged, the worst insult I could have given him, and then my father turned and went out this door, slamming it behind him, and I saw my mother, still turned toward the stove, flinch, and I put my empty plate in the sink and mumbled thanks to her and went out this door also, and stepped into my Volkswagen, and drove away.

It's a terrible thing to have been the lucky one. And even worse for that luck to have led you to an insolence and arrogance that you will spend the rest of your life regretting. I did not even have to work that day—I had made a plan to pick up my blue-eyed Wellesley girl whose hair smelled like oranges and take her to an abandoned quarry, where we made love the rest of the day on some rocks in the sun and then, once it began to rain, in the backseat of my German car.

And it is a terrible thing, too, for the pleasure of sex to be poisoned forever by the guilt of one day.

I leap up, rub my cold hands on the legs of my jeans, and start walking across the yard to the road. My limbs are weak from caffeine, and the breath coming out of my lungs burns. At the road I stop and look in both directions: up-hill into the woods where it dead-ends; downhill toward Jane's farm and the road that leads away. "Goddamnit," I whimper, but only the birds can hear. It's a spot I stood in many times as a boy and, later, as a teenager, a place where you can see the clean streak of Silver Creek and beyond it the gentle swell and tip of Monadnock's breast-shaped peak, a place that offers the gift and promise of distance. South of me I can see Jane's husband driving east on his shiny new John Deere across what we always called Stink Pasture for the way it smelled of skunkweed and wet cow shit, and I begin walking, almost running, down the road toward that tractor for a reason I can't explain. From the crest of the hill I see Jane's house, and I pause to look at the new white vinyl siding on the old structure, making it look tidy and durable, and the blue-gray double-wide a quarter mile downhill, a Chrysler parked in its front yard, and then I catch a glimpse of red hair through the window of the barn and for a moment I am fifteen again and it is Jane—Jane, a year older than I, with long, colt-ish legs and full lips and a way of teaching boys things in haylofts that they will never in all their lives be able to thank her appropriately for—but then I realize that Jane's hair is chopped short now and losing its color so it must be her daughter's hair I see through the dusty glass, and I slow down.

My father never spoke of what happened, so it is my mother's and my sisters' stories that I have pieced to-gether into history. My mother told me later, much later, that after I left that day my father came into the house and said, "Get the other boy."

My mother turned to him. "Jake, he can't."

"He will," my father said. So my mother went upstairs and woke Ross, who dressed and ate the biscuit my mother handed him and followed my father out into the field.

My mother stayed in the house for an hour, washing the breakfast dishes and starting bread, then went outside to feed the chickens. Back inside she woke my sisters and told them they had to go to the field too, to help get the hay in. They woke up slow, took their time getting dressed. The sun by that point had already disappeared behind some clouds, and there was a thick, dark bank rolling in from the west.

At around ten my mother filled a jug with cold spring water and walked out toward the farthest hayfield, where my brother and father worked, the field just visible to my left now, if I turn my head to see it. My sisters were still in the kitchen eating breakfast. My mother could hear my father shouting before she could see the field, and so she walked quickly. When she got there she saw my father leap off the tractor and yell at Ross, who had a bale in his arms, which he was slowly and painfully trying to roll toward the truck. Dark, charcoal clouds gathered in the sky, and my mother felt a drop of rain on her cheek. My father must have felt one too, for at that moment he looked up toward the sky and yelled "Goddamnit!" to my brother, who was at that point straining with his upper arms and torso, while balancing on his unstable legs, to lift the bale up toward the back of the truck. "Goddamn useless!" my father yelled. And my mother told me that forever after those words could be heard in her head if she allowed them to ring there.

I turn my head to the east, toward the field I have tried not to look at for twenty years: Stark's pasture. A flat field gently sloping, a long birch in its center. I cannot move, looking at that just-visible field. I kneel down, there in the grass at the edge of the road, and feel the mud soak through the thin denim knees of my jeans. I put my face close to that mud and think for a moment I may stay there forever, and then I hop up and rub my face with my sleeve and start walking, as fast as I can, until I reach the edge of the Cole, no, Clement barnyard. My breath is uneven; my legs shake. No one is in sight, and the yard smells of tractor oil and cow shit and hay, and the combination is a smell as familiar as a damp wool coat or Helen's just-washed hair. I go to the barn and pause in the doorway and look into the darkness my eyes have yet to adjust to. I can hear a shovel in the far end of the barn, and the radio is playing someone who sounds like Reba McEntire but probably is not, as it's been a good fifteen years since I last listened to this station.

It was this barn my mother ran to for help. I don't know the details of that moment—whether she encountered Jane's father in the doorway and told him to call or whether she found the phone in the house herself. And

I don't know what her face looked like, or whether the words she said to the operator were garbled by terror or whether they came out matter-of-fact and plain, as shock will sometimes make them come. I know that the local firemen were the first to show up, and that they drove out into the field in their red truck, and that one of them, a friend of mine, knelt in the damp and freshly cut hay where my father had lain my brother's body, and checked his pulse, and I know that the fireman did not look in my mother's eyes when he told her that her son was dead. Adelaide told me all of that. She had just been cresting the hill with Dell when my father screamed at my brother to move his "goddamn legs," and so Ross had spread his legs and put his chest up against the bale and wrapped his arms around it and leaned his head back, trying in vain to heave the bale four feet up onto the top of the stack, and as he did so he screamed, a scream that was not a scream of effort but of anger and anguish, and still the bale did not make it even halfway up. And then my sisters watched as my father, in a rare moment of acquiescence, saw the raw misery of his deformed son and so called out, "Stop," and said, for perhaps the first time, his youngest son's name—"Ross, stop"—and my sisters watched as my brother either didn't hear my father over the noise of the tractor or ignored him and continued to lift and scream, and my sisters stood there, still watching, as our brother's screaming suddenly stopped and his face went white and his body, like a doll's, began to slowly tip sideways, and the bale fell by his side, and they stood there at the top of the hill, half blinded by the soft rain that now fell, as our mother dropped her jug of water and ran to him, and as my father stood there unmoving in terror and disbelief, before running toward his son, his son with the weak heart, whom he picked up and carried to the shelter of that single birch tree. It was his weak heart. That weak heart he was born with that did him in.

That is when our mother left for the Cole barn. This very same barn whose doorframe I now kneel in, dizzy, my hands shaking, spitting up what has risen in my throat into the hay and dust and dirt that has collected in the corner of the doorway. My head throbs, my legs ache, and I think, for a strange and elated moment, that I may die.

That is when I notice her sneakers. I lift my eyes and there is Rachel, redheaded, the girl with her mother's hair, standing in front of me, eyes wide, lips parted, as if I am some feral animal she has just come upon.

"Are you okay?" she asks.

I lean my hand for a moment against the wood of the doorway and put my head against my arm and whisper—it is all I can manage—"I think so. Yes. I think so. Okay."

The girl just stands there, watching me. "Do you need some water?"

"Yes," I say. "That would be good."

"Wait here," she says, and goes to the tap in the milk room and comes back with a Mason jar full of water.

"Here, take this," she says, and I dust off my hands and

take a sip of the water. It is so cold, it makes my teeth hurt, and it is the cleanest thing I have ever tasted.

"Thank you," I say.

"Sure," she says, still standing there, looking at me as if I am crazy, or drunk, which I might still be, but she doesn't look scared anymore, or like she will go away, and I don't want her to, and am surprised to find myself thinking that.

"Need anything else?" she asks.

"No. I don't think so." I manage to smile at her. "I don't know what happened."

"It's okay."

She smiles at me then, an old-hearted and gracious smile, for which I'm grateful.

Then she shifts her feet. "You want to come see the calves? I was just cleaning their stalls." And like that there is a way forward. All I have to do is nod, and she leads me through the milk room and down a hallway to a small room with one window. It's one big stall and in it are three calves, each no more than a few days old. They stand on shaky legs and look up at me with wide, wet eyes, and when I hold my pale hands toward them they lick my fingers, their tongues rough as beach sand, and their dark eyes are so full of trust, as is this Rachel, who has brought me into this room, that I think I may foolishly cry. But I do not cry. Instead I think of Helen, and wish she were here with me, wish she could see these calves lick my hands and let them lick hers, wish I could start over, but I let that thought pass, and simply kneel in the clean sawdust Rachel has just laid down, and let the small creatures lick the salt off my face and my arms and my hands.

"Sweet, huh?" Rachel says, and I nod, and then I stand up and look once again at her slate-blue eyes, and reach my hand out and touch her shoulder, and then turn and leave the barn and walk back up the road toward my own farm. I pause for a moment in that road with my arms at my side and close my eyes and think that maybe life offers us more than one chance to survive, or more than one way to be lucky, and then I keep walking, toward the place where I was born, toward the place where too many of my loved ones died, and from this angle the house and barn somehow look less solid, less violent, less permanent, their half ruin letting in some new kind of light, and the rivers, which at dawn looked like veins, now look like rivers, carrying cold water toward some larger, yet-to-be determined home.

"Ross," I say out loud. I haven't said his name in such a long time. "Ross," my voice broken, too loud, an animal in there. "I'm sorry. I'm so bloody sorry." And he answers. His body everywhere. The field the grass the mud the barn.

9

THE LONG ROAD
TURNS TO JOY

Apple conceived in a field in early September 1987, the year she turned nineteen. She had named herself that after moving to Vicksburg, where hundred-year-old apple trees grew around all the old houses and sometimes appeared, gnarled and unruly, deep in the woods. The night she conceived she lay in the wet grass and watched the sparks from a nearby bonfire transform into a meteor shower that suddenly appeared above her. The man she slept with was a long-fingered married guitar player, passing through, but all of that was unimportant. When she found out she was pregnant, a month later, she wrote in her journal that a spirit had moved through her that night like a warm wind. Sparrow, she named her boy, for the bird that sang outside her cabin window the June he was born.

Now, eighteen years later, Apple sits in her trailer, which perches on a hill above a large farmhouse. It's late December, a week before Christmas, and she rests her sock feet on top of the gas heater. Her feet are cold. The trailer is cold; the trailer is always cold. The house below used to belong to a woman named Cora, whom Apple took care of when she was dying, but now it belongs to a couple of thirty-year-old artists—a dancer and a trapeze artist—who rented the trailer to Apple and Sparrow two years ago. Sparrow was a junior in high school then, and the man and woman had stared intently and with curiosity into Sparrow's eyes. He was—is—a beautiful boy, deep, dark eyes and an overly serious look for his age, and most people find themselves drawn to him. "It would be nice to have some young blood around," the man had said, and Sparrow smiled and told them he looked forward to being somewhere quiet, somewhere without too many neighbors. The couple looked at each other and smiled, and Apple had felt proud. They were good landlords. It was a good place to live. She liked having Cora's ghost around—her efficiency and kindness. Apple was happy here. Until the day after graduation when Sparrow came home and told her he had joined the marines. It's the things you can't imagine, she thought then, that sneak up and knife you from behind.

The trailer has a large picture window that faces the

HALF WILD

field, and from where Apple sits, looking out, she can see the hill slope away toward the road and, beyond that, a bank of trees and, to her left, ninety feet downhill, the two-hundred-year-old farmhouse where the artists live. The barn that used to stand across from it burned to the ground not long before Cora died. The ashes from that fire are nearly gone; the grass grows abundant. Apple often finds herself watching the house and the couple who live in it without intending to. In summer they weed their large vegetable garden together, the woman (the trapeze artist) in a bikini top and a short cotton skirt, the man (the dancer), shirtless in cut-off jeans. Sometimes they do yoga in the yard. They are both thin and tan and have enough money to buy themselves this house and a brand-new four-wheel-drive Volvo, and to Apple they always seem happy. Now she watches as they come out of the house, dressed in snow pants and thick down parkas. They grab bright plastic sleds from the porch and hike up the hill in front of Apple's trailer. When they get to the top they lie down on their sleds and shoot down the old cow field together. At the bottom, before reaching the trees, they bail out of the sleds and throw themselves into the snow. Apple can hear their shrieks and laughter; she can see them crawl toward each other and start groping each other there in the snow in their big down jackets. Her eyes are still that good. Apple has been single, barring a few errant nights, for eighteen years.

Now she stands and goes to her bookshelf where she

141

keeps the letters Sparrow sends her. In the most recent one—received three months ago—he describes mountain caves and the bombed-out houses where they sleep in the mountains of Afghanistan; he describes fields of poppies and watermelon. He says they run into those fields, break the watermelon open, stick their faces inside, and devour the sweet fruit. *The only fresh thing we've eaten in six fucking months,* he writes. And then, *Hey Apple— more socks?* He never mentions guns or killing or fighting. Once a month Apple sends packages of clean white socks. There is no such thing as laundry, and they are on their feet in those leather boots fifteen, sometimes sixteen hours a day. Socks, Sparrow has told her, are the heroin of his brigade.

Once every few months he calls. It is always early, three or four in the morning. The connection is never good, and he can never talk for more than a few minutes, but for Apple, shivering there in the dark of the trailer in her nightgown, bare feet on linoleum, Sparrow's voice coming through that line is the most grace-filled thing she has ever known. He never mentions guns or killing or fighting, but it is all over the news.

Apple puts the letter down and goes to the kitchen to start dinner. She pulls carrots and kale out of the refrigerator, pours brown rice and water into a pan. She works as a cashier at the health food store in Nelson and has always eaten well—rice and beans, vegetables and tofu, unrefined sugars. She has come a long way from the house outside Cleveland where she grew up: all that meat and potatoes, cake out of boxes, and Jell-O molds. A long way from her God- and husband-fearing mother. And yet, like her mother, she now lives and cooks alone. Which is why she finds herself, after all these years, calling her mother more often than she used to.

They don't talk about anything important, but Apple is surprised to find herself comforted by the sound of her mother's thin voice across all that distance. The last time her mother visited was sixteen years ago; Apple was living in a converted chicken coop, and Sparrow was two. When her mother asked where the ladies' room was and Apple pointed to the outhouse nestled between some pines, her mother said, "Oh dear," and rented herself a motel room. The next day she told Apple she should get herself a mirror: "Don't you care how you *look*?" Apple had looked down at her body then: her full hips and flat feet and small, pointy breasts under loose cotton. She has a picture of herself from back then tacked to the window frame above her sink, and every time she sees it she is surprised at the raw beauty of her young face. Yes, she hadn't said: she cared.

But that was a long time ago. Now her father is dead and her mother talks about food and her sick parents and her neighbors. "How is our boy?" she asks toward the end of the conversation, and Apple tells her about the most recent letter from Sparrow, or reports that she has heard nothing at all. "Well, God is with him," her mother always says. "God knows best." And every time Apple hangs up the phone, she cries.

Apple peels the carrots. It is the strangest thing she has known, to have a son at war. For years she has hung a poster above her bed that says VISUALIZE WHIRLED PEAS. When Sparrow was a boy she taught him to leave spider webs undisturbed, to catch mice in Havahart traps and wasps in jars. The small bookshelf in the trailer holds every book Thich Naht Hanh has written. Taped to the wall above her kitchen sink is his reminder to *Breathe peace;* to the wall next to her bed she has tacked his lines: *No birth, no death, no coming, no going. The long road turns to joy.*

Sparrow was a good teenager. He never did too many drugs or drank too much or went off any deep end like Apple had always feared. She wasn't sure if he had any close friends, but he liked his teachers and his teachers liked him. He would be going to the state college in the fall. He took art classes and made Apple ceramic cups and bowls for Christmas and her birthday. On weekend nights he took Apple's Subaru and went to parties but never got too messed up. If he drank, he spent the night; that was her rule. In the morning he would come home and they would sit in the trailer drinking coffee together and he would tell her about drinking games and skinny-dipping and other kids who did things that were stupid, and Apple thought then that she was in the clear, that she had done everything right, that all those years of teaching peace and love and simplicity had been the right way to raise a child, the right way to mother, that if the world only did it like she had done it, the world would be a better, more humane place: without hunger, without massacres, without war.

He told her the day after graduation. Apple sat at the edge of the field waiting for him, the hardcover copy of *Leaves of Grass* gift-wrapped beside her. It was the book his English teacher had recommended. Sparrow pulled into the driveway in Apple's rusted Subaru and came and sat down next to her. He picked a blade of timothy and stuck it between his lips. "Apple," he said, not looking at her. He smelled like beer and looked like he'd slept in a field somewhere.

"Yeah?"

"I have something to tell you."

In that instant Apple had imagined all sorts of possible declarations: a girl knocked up, a one-way ticket to California, a drug felony or a speeding ticket or a night in jail. But never what came next. Apple had never imagined the cut of those words, the nausea that sliced through every vein in a heartbeat.

Before she could say anything he gave her two reasons. One, he told her, his pale fingers shaking, was that a war was being fought in the name of freedom and justice and if people were going to die for it, he might as well too.

He didn't look at her as he said it; his voice caught in his throat, too loud. It sounded like something he had read in a pamphlet and memorized. And, he had said, this time glancing at Apple, his lower lip beginning to tremble, they were going to pay for his college. "How else were you going to do it?" In that instant Apple felt her life unearthing itself like a flock of starlings taking off from a field. Every one of those birds was her mistake. Hers.

The light shifts in the trailer and Apple hears the door at the big house slam. She can't help herself—she goes to the picture window and looks down the hill. The husband and wife are brushing the snow off each other's pants and jackets with a straw broom. The man goes to the woodpile and fills his arms with a load of wood; the woman holds the door open for him, and they walk inside together. Lights come on in half a dozen windows. Apple goes back to her kitchen and throws the chopped carrots and kale into the pan.

She likes cooking without lights on. It's a new thing, not something she did with Sparrow in the house. When he was there she would turn on all the lights and cut vegetables at the table where he did his homework. Not that he needed her help—he always did well in school—but because she wanted to learn what he was learning and because she wanted to share his life with him. She often read his assigned English books so they could talk about them afterward. She read *The Catcher in the Rye* and *Great Expectations* and *As I Lay Dying*. "You can read your own books," Sparrow said once, but Apple told him she liked reading with him; she had been high most of her high school years, or having sex in the backseats of cars. She secretly imagined herself starting over with Sparrow. His English teacher had told his class that *As I Lay Dying* was the greatest American poem of the twentieth century, and Apple read it a second time with that in mind, though she still isn't sure she completely understands what it's about.

The rice water starts to boil and Apple turns it down to a simmer, stirs the vegetables. The clock on the stove and the stereo light create a pleasant glow. Outside, the sky looks like the worn navy on a velvet dress Apple once saw Cora wearing, mottled here and there with stars. It's not even five, but in December it gets dark so early.

In sixth grade Sparrow asked if they could move somewhere warmer, lighter, somewhere like Florida. "Why?" Apple asked, and he shrugged and said he didn't like the cold. But Apple knew he did like the cold; he liked sledding and making snow angels, and he liked to spend time outside by himself. That week Sparrow's teacher called to talk; she said the boys in Sparrow's class were calling him "Birdie." She asked, "Does Sparrow like having his hair long, or would he prefer a haircut?" She said he often pulled his hair over his eyes and didn't take off his winter parka when he came inside. When Apple asked Sparrow about his hair and about the jacket and about school he said he was fine. It was fine. He just wanted somewhere warmer, that's all.

Apple brings her bowl of food to the chair in front of the gas heater. It's the only place in the trailer she likes to be now—a rocking chair draped with sheepskin—and when she sits there rocking she sometimes feels like an old woman and that feeling comforts her; the pressure to live a striking life recedes. Sometimes Apple looks down at her long, slender legs and is surprised that she is not even forty. Lots of women her age are just having babies.

A car pulls into the driveway below, and Apple watches two people climb out. They are just shadows against the snow, but Apple can make out their shapes by the light that streams through the windows: both elegantly thin. The couple goes to the porch and another car pulls up. Apple remembers it is Saturday, almost Christmas: the time of year for parties. Two more shadows climb out of the second car and go toward the house. The front door opens to reveal the trapeze artist standing in the doorway in a red cocktail dress and black high-heeled shoes. She laughs and embraces the silhouettes and they embrace her and then they all step inside, the door closing behind them. Apple looks down at her own clothes: a favorite wool sweater full of holes and a pair of jeans. She wonders for a moment if she should turn a light on in the trailer so they won't think she is sleeping or depressed or sitting in the dark, watching them. Her Subaru is parked outside her door, and if they see it there, they will know she is home, without lights on, but why on earth would they look up the hill and wonder? They are having a party!

Sometimes she feels like a god up here, looking out and down, and thinks how lonely it must be to be a god.

Sparrow used to tell her to go out. "You should go dancing. Or to a concert," he would say. Once: "You're still pretty, you know," and Apple had thought, looking into those deep and serious eyes, how happy he was going to make some woman someday. She had slept with lots of men but had not loved one of them. "The best thing you can do for your children," she had heard someone say at a wedding, "is love their mother." But who had loved her? Apple had looked at Sparrow then and pulled him against her body in a long and awkward hug, which he pulled away from gently.

Inside the house down the hill the dancer lights a candelabra, and the guests gather around the table and sit down. They pour wine and raise their glasses to toast something; they laugh and smile. A month ago Sparrow's company slept for a week in a bombed-out house without food, only fresh water dropped by plane. Every day she went to the library and looked at pictures on CNN's website: marines behind mud walls holding machine guns, marines playing with chickens, marines dashing across bullet-sprayed fields. One of the bodies in camouflage looked like Sparrow from the side, but Apple couldn't tell for sure: an all-American-looking boy. When Apple thinks of her child holding a gun, she feels the world fall out from under her. She thinks of car accidents and police brutality and childhood leukemia and the seagulls dead from oil spills in Alaska or the Gulf of Mexico. She's afraid, sometimes, to breathe. She hasn't washed her hair for days.

Apple finishes her food and puts her bowl in the sink. She'll do the dishes in the morning. She won't mind; she likes washing dishes. It's what she will do after she washes the dishes that worries her. The *now* to contend with. Thich Nhat Hanh says our true home is the here and now. He says, *Breathe! You are alive.* Apple sits back down in her rocker and wishes, as she sometimes wishes at night now, that she still drank. Just a little. Not like her father, but just a little bit of wine. She says the words out loud: "Breathe, you are alive." She repeats them in her head as she closes her eyes and practices her breathing.

When she opens her eyes again there is motion in the big house below: people clearing plates, clearing glasses, carrying them through the door that leads to the kitchen. Then they are lifting the tablecloth off the table, moving chairs, moving the table itself. Apple can no longer see the table, and she is wondering at what kind of dinner party people disassemble the table, when the couples come back into the room and start dancing. They dance beautifully. The men wrap their right arms around the women; their left hands cup the women's slender fingers. The trapeze artist twirls under her husband's arm, and her red dress spins out around her like an inverted poppy. Another woman is wearing blue jeans and a top that looks like lingerie. She and her partner dance with their knees bent, shaking their elbows and hips and heads. The third couple holds each other so tight that from where Apple sits they look like one large person, spinning. The sky above the house is filled with stars, and it is a beautiful thing, all that stardust lighting up the snow, the people on earth dancing.

She hasn't been to a party in a long time. When Sparrow was five Apple got stoned and lost him. Or he lost her. All she remembers is a bonfire at the edge of Sunset Lake, people drumming, kids running loose, a woman singing Tracy Chapman's "Fast Car," a joint being passed her way. She remembers thinking this is how it would be in other parts of the world—the Amazon, Africa, an earlier America—kids barefoot in the dark, their own tribe, their own wilderness. She remembers feeling happy and not-alone there at the fire, singing along, her body swaying, the warm night fragrant with pollen. She remembers a short and muscular and handsome man playing a fiddle; she remembers he had been the one to pass her the joint. After that was a blur: a child screaming somewhere in the woods. A woman calling out, "Where are the kids?" and people running this way and that. Then a man's voice calling out "Got him! He's fine," and a wet boy, not hers, being dragged out of the water. His mother wrapped him in sweaters and jackets, and his father carried him to the fire. The mother started singing in the boy's ear, and the father smiled, kissed him. *Fine, baby, you're fine,* he sang, a mantra of comfort. But Apple couldn't find Sparrow. "Sparrow?" she called into the woods, toward the water. "Sparrow? Where are you?" No one noticed her prowling around out there in the woods by the water's edge, stoned. No one heard her calling. It wasn't until what seemed much later, after the lake-wet child's hair had dried and his limbs had stopped shaking, after people had finished celebrating his rescue, that Apple heard the whimpering. She followed the sound until she found Sparrow, crouched against the wall of an empty lake cabin, a long way from the fire. There was a long, thin scratch on his left shin, a trickle of blood. "Mama," he had said, looking up at her, his face wet with tears. Apple sat down next to him and wiped the blood with her skirt, then reached for his hand and held it. She couldn't find words to say. Her legs felt too long, her hands small as a child's. She sat that way until her head felt steady, until her heart calmed, until he stopped making that awful sound. That was the last time she got stoned.

A side door of the big house opens, letting light spill out onto the porch for a moment, then closes. A shadow floats across the lit yard, then disappears into darkness. Apple wonders if someone is a closet smoker, or is making a phone call in secret, but that kind of deception feels unfitting to these people and their happiness. Inside, all she can see is the couple wrapped together, tilting their heads back and away from each other, their bodies still entwined, still spinning, as if they are a plant growing outward.

The last time she spoke to Sparrow was twenty-three days ago at three fifteen in the morning, a few days after they cleared the road and his company returned to food and water. She leapt out of bed and stumbled to the phone, picking it up with her breathless "hello," and then there was the pause she wanted, the pause she is always hoping for, the pause that tells her someone is calling long, long distance. It always feels a little like communicating with the stars. But all she could hear was Sparrow's voice saying a few muffled words she couldn't understand, her name—*Apple*—rising like a question, and the crackling snap of the connection ending. Then it was just the dark trailer, and the refrigerator buzzing, and her cold feet on linoleum. Since then the fighting has escalated. It is all over the news: insurgent attacks; marines dying in helicopter crashes; marines dying from friendly fire. She is almost sure she saw him in a photo on a website a week ago: a company in the mountains, mud-spattered, in combat, and at the far edge of the frame a boy, Sparrow-like, too thin, running.

Apple closes her eyes and does the breathing thing she has taught herself to do: long inhale through the nose, count to three, exhale through parted lips. She breathes, and as she does so she erases those pictures from her mind. Her heartbeat slows, her limbs relax.

She learned a lot that year she took care of Cora as she was dying. *The snow,* Cora had said, her voice barely audible, her thin hand in Apple's. *Oh how I love the snow.*

Apple feels her toes on the heater, her long body in its chair. One, two, three, exhale. It is working. She is growing sleepy. She is almost asleep, and in her half dream she is floating across that open, snow-covered field, spinning like the dancers down the hill. The refrigerator comes on, rattles, goes off. The wind picks up outside. Her boy is a small thing, suckling on her breast, and she is sure-of-heart for him. They are there by that abandoned cabin near the lake, her arms wrapped around him, his blood drying on her skirt, and she is whispering, *Fine, baby, you're fine.* He is flying back over the ocean, toward her. He meets her somewhere in that dull sky, up above the field.

A knock at the door and Apple startles. She opens her eyes and feels a momentary jolt of excitement. Sparrow? It is an old instinct. But the knock comes again and she is suddenly fully awake. *A knock at the door.* Her stomach dips, acid swarming. Isn't this how it happens? Two retired marines, parking at the bottom of the hill and walking up the snow-covered road. Or just a couple of kids in their Blue Dress uniforms, not much older than Sparrow, death already in their eyes. Either way, two bodies standing there in the dark and cold, eyes turned down.

No lights, she thinks. No lights. They don't have to know I'm here. If this is it, I cannot take it, I cannot hear it, I would rather live in the dark than know. Another knock but Apple doesn't move: body stiff, limbs tingling, metal taste on her tongue. Breathe! She wants to will herself back to the dream: that flying, that field, those arms. *No birth, no death, no coming, no going.* The knocking stops and does not come again: silence, and that eerie light of the moon streaking now across the room.

A few minutes pass and she gets up, walks quietly to the door. She cannot feel her feet or hands. She thinks of her mother's sturdy God, of that night at the lake and all her failures. She opens the door. A cold wind hits her face. She blinks, squints, inhales.

At first all she can see is the snow that has begun to fall: drifting shadows. Then, the gray streak moving down the driveway, a figure against all that white. A whimper escapes her lips that sounds, in her own ears, like a cat dying. Watermelons, mud, boys in fields.

But there is a skirt, swaying. Her eyes are adjusting. A woman. A skirt under a down jacket, the swing of female hips: the trapeze artist's red dress. Apple releases the air out of her lungs. Her eyes fall to the step below her. There is something there, a plate covered in tinfoil. She reaches out and brushes the tinfoil off with her toe: pie. A piece of pie. Even in this light she can see the juices, pooling in concentric rings. A beautiful slice of berry pie.

Apple's limbs start to shake before the tears come. She

can think of times people have given her money, loaned her cars, helped stack her wood, but this is so surprising: this woman, this skirt, this gift.

She stands in the open doorway, cold air filling up the trailer, snot and tears running down her face, her body heaving in sobs, and she does not feel cold. She does not feel cold here at the top of the hill, watching it snow, immersed in the magnificent silence that comes with falling snow. He will come back, she says, and believes it. He will come back. *The long road turns to joy.*

10

LOVE BIRDS

The morning of the day Tub died we went out driving around looking at houses. We took the back roads we grew up on: Butterfield, Stark, Stickney Brook, Cowpath 40. You could say it was a hobby of ours. This driving. Looking. Every time we drove one of those old familiar roads something was different—a new house popped up, or an addition, or an old house sold, or an old house torn down. We'd been doing it for some forty-seven years together. "Could sell our brains to some historical society when we die, Tub," I said.

Tub chuckled. "Worth a buck or two," he said. "Maybe."

Dying both was and was not a joke between us. It seemed to come up at least once or twice a day, without us even meaning to. "Not like I'm gonna go jump off a bridge," one of us would say. Or, "Well, when I die don't go complaining I didn't treat you nice." Or, "Well, kill me why don't ya." It was a joke because Tub and I were always jokers. It wasn't a joke because of Tub's heart and because it seemed that what neither of us was saying out loud was spurting out every other goddamn place like in a broken fuel line. I guess those holes are where the truth gets out.

And that day was just like any other. It was mid-November, the air blue as a robin's egg. We didn't work on Sundays, so we got into our thirty-year-old green diesel Rabbit and drove around. We brought a thermos of coffee, ham sandwiches, and a couple beers, which we propped between our legs. It was cold out, "cold enough to freeze them titties," Tub said that morning as we walked out the door.

"Ha," I said, "what's left of them."

That's Tub and I: meant for each other. We went east on Stickney, then turned left onto Lake, then crossed the green metal bridge that goes up onto the ridge above Silver Creek. We passed the old Adams farmhouse that got bought in the seventies sometime by some hippies and turned into a commune.

"Little house on the prairie here," Tub said, and I took a swig of my beer and pinched his thigh.

We passed Bud Williams's trailer and garage where he fixes school buses. His girlfriend, Shelley, was out in the yard putting leaves on her flower beds, her bare legs under her dress fat as watermelons. Tub honked and waved, and Shelley looked up and waved back. "First time I see that girl work outside in her life," Tub said.

"Girl," I said. "She's probably fifty."

"Not as perty as my girl," Tub said, and leaned over and pinched my wrinkly, seventy-some-year-old all-bone thigh.

We took the car down Auger Hole road and turned left onto Butterfield. Tub finished his beer, and I reached into the backseat and handed him another. Only a few leaves still clung to the trees, and it hurt me a little in the chest to see them hanging on and shaking like that, all brown and ropey. We passed a hippie house tucked up against the bank of the river, shingles and glass everywhere, a stained-glass window and a falling-in porch. We used to bet on how long each of them hippies would last. Most of them didn't, or they moved out of their little shacks and built themselves houses their daddies paid for and got themselves jobs, or they turned the shacks into big glass houses. The men Tub would chuckle at: *Goddamn hippies,* he would say. But he loved the young pretty women with the long hair. He told me it was for business that he was so friendly, but I know Tub well enough to know he was charmed like any other good man by a pretty woman's smile.

He was charmed by me, too. Sixteen in a truck, pretty then as any of these young back-to-the-land women are, but I knew how to rope a horse and build a shed and strip the bark off a tree. Now I've been good and weathered by sun and wind and I know I'm missing one front tooth, but it's okay. Tub loves me just the same. That I know.

At the top of Farm Hill Road, past the Maises' and some goat-farming ladies' place, Tub surprised me by pulling the car over on the side of the road. I knew his old family cemetery was around there somewhere, but I couldn't remember quite where. Tub got out and took a leak in a ditch. I got out too and stretched my arms up above my head, and then he headed into the woods where there's a break between the stone walls and I followed. "Say hello to the corpses," Tub said. I just nodded. Like I said, it's what we don't say where the truth slips out.

It's not far through the woods: a half mile at the most. Just when you start to think you're lost you can make out the stone wall that surrounds the graves. 1790, the dates on the first stones say. Quite a few have the last name Stark, like my Tub. Their stones are falling over this way and that in the leaves, like some people's teeth I know.

"Looks like our teeth, Tub!" I called out from where I stood, looking down at them this way and that. Tub grinned, showing me his.

He rubbed his thick fingers over the names and started shouting some of them out loud; Constance, Ezekial, Zipporah, Desire. The lucky ones died at birth or of old age. The unlucky, midway. There's lots of ways we could have died if we stopped to think of it: one widow-maker limb, one dumb cut, the horse's sled overturning in a rut. I thought for a moment of Tub's heart, and then I put that thought away like cold cash locked up good.

Tub sat on a stone with his hands on his knees. He pulled his half-empty beer out of his pocket and took a slug, then looked up at the sky. He was still handsome as the devil: pink cheeks and hands like a bear. I pulled out our ham sandwiches and sat down on the wall next to Tub, and we ate. The wind bit at my ears, and I pulled my coat up around them. Tub, he moved closer, put his arm around my waist. I could hear the sound of his chewing in my ears, he was so close. He smelled dank like old skin and sweet like apples. My man. My man with the way with women and horses.

When Tub was around the horses he would get quiet, his breath deeper, move slow and steady and calm as a leaf in pond water. He knew just what would make those horses spook, and he was always looking ahead for it, seeing it before they would, pulling on their reins ever so slightly, touching their flank so they would know even in that moment who was in charge. When he spoke to them his voice was low and strong and he didn't waste words, just said what they needed to hear and then they'd do it. It was a beautiful thing to see, even for me. "Women and animals," I've said to him forever. "You know how to work them both." And Tub, he'd just show me his handsome set of yellow teeth and flash his devil's grin.

But that day he was feeling something different. I could see it in the way he was moving his fingers—rubbing them back and forth on his jeans. The doctor said his heart was bad because of diet—that Tub should stop eating red meat and drinking beer, but I said he had a weak heart because he has always had a weak heart—for women and for animals and for woods and most especially for me. But that doesn't mean that heart didn't keep me up at night. His breathing was heavier than it used to be, his face veering on a shade of plum.

It started one day last September while Tub was delivering wood to a woman on Butler Road, a big ranch house with a pool and an attached garage. Tub dumped the wood where he had always dumped it, and then this Barbara Stokes comes running out of the house screaming and yelling something about a rhododendron and Tub thought *Somebody's tendon?* Like someone must be hurt there in the house and so he ran toward the door all worried until he realized this woman was upset at *him* and she was squawking like a chicken he said and flapping her groomed arms all around and finally she calmed down enough for him to figure out that he had dumped the two cords of wood right on this lady's newly planted bed of rhododendrons.

That's when you know there's a part of them that doesn't really respect you.

That night after dinner Tub's heart began to hurt. After that it hurt him every day, though he wouldn't make a fuss over it. Like that morning amongst those stones. "Look at them crows," Tub said, and he pointed to the edge of the clearing where two big ones sat in the top branches of a hemlock tree.

"Love birds," I said, pinching Tub's thigh. "Crows are birds that mate for life."

"Damn racket hounds."

"Damn ugly love birds," I said, and giggled, and Tub he turned toward me and said, "Least they ain't missing their teeth," and we both giggled some more.

After that day at Barbara Stokes's he hadn't thought too much about his heart at first, just went out with the flashlight to the lean-to and fed the horses like he always did and gave them fresh water, and when he came back in he was breathing heavy and kind of holding his chest, and I said, "Tub, honey, you don't look too goddamn well," and he said it was nothing to worry about so we just climbed into bed early like that, him all quiet and me lying next to him wide awake as a buzzard.

The next day it wasn't better, so I said, "Tub, you and me going to Doc Whatsihoosit." Tub said okay, which I knew was bad. We walked down the trail and got into our VW Rabbit and drove to the doctor, who said sure enough, Tub's arteries were mostly blocked and that he was lucky he come in when he did and that Tub should have bypass surgery, and when Tub said, "No goddamn way in hell!" the doc said well then you're gonna have to change some things about the way you do your living. No red meat, no drink, no hard work for a few months. Slow and easy walks are good. Clearly Doc didn't know my Tub like I do. And, the doctor said, there's a good chance you'll die.

So there we were, sitting looking at dead people's stones in the middle of the day facing winter low on cash and grain and something else too. Spunk, maybe. All that summer, despite Tub's efforts to help, I had to get the firewood out and split and into the truck by myself, which meant we only sold half as much. Tub could drive the truck still and do the delivering, but he couldn't be tying the chains around the logs and he couldn't be working Shoehorn and Jake and he couldn't even lift the logs onto the splitter. It's okay—I know how to work the muscles in my short arms and legs—but it wasn't good for Tub to see me doing all that work and him just sitting by holding his chest and breathing hard. "It's okay, Tub," I had said to him a few days earlier. "You're still the best man in fifty miles square." But that didn't seem to heat him up much. He just grunted and said, "Sorry, Vi," looking like he'd swallowed some rusty piece of metal.

"Ready to hit the road?" he said. The wind had picked up even more, so I nodded and lifted myself up from the stone wall with a little grunt.

"So long, old folks," I said toward the loose gray stones. Tub's dead people didn't say anything back to us, but the crows in the trees made a racket.

Tub kicked some leaves in the direction of the stones. "Don't go running off on us now," he said to his dead folks. Then he spit into the leaves by his feet and took my hand and we walked back to the car like that.

We climbed in and started her up. I opened the thermos of coffee and poured some into the Styrofoam cups we kept on the floor. We sat there for a while at the side of the road with the motor running and sipped the black coffee. It warmed my tongue and the back of my throat and my belly. No cars passed. Just Tub and me, sitting there like that, drinking coffee and admiring the view.

We emptied the thermos and Tub started driving home. He took some of the skinny back roads we like going on; Turnpike, Old Farm, Fox. They're roads we'd known our whole lives. Roads we'd seen change like our own faces. You could map our whole lives on these little two-bit dirt roads and not have to go farther than forty square miles. I don't say that like I think I'm missing something.

At the corner of Turnpike and Fox the trees open up into a field and there's a view past Round Mountain all the way to Monadnock in New Hampshire. Tub pulled the car over there, and we climbed out and stood with our backs against it and looked out at the hills. We've logged half of the woods we can see. Lenny Whitman owned this field, then Otie Hollows, then a fella from down south for just a few years, and now some silver-haired college professor who lives alone, quiet, like the rest of us. Little family-tree maps of who owned what back as far as I know for every piece of ground I see. There were no houses in view from where we stood, and I was happy for that. But at the far corner you could see where Rich Miller had sold large chunks of Whiskey Mountain—my cousin Sugar's unowned haunt—for subdivisions fifteen years ago.

"Goddamn," Tub said.

"Horse-ass," I said.

"We should go down there with dynamite."

"Take the horses in there and have them shit all over the new floors," I said, giggling. Tub snorted and looked at me, and for a moment the fear disappeared from his round face, and he came over and picked me up like he sometimes does—I'm barely five feet tall, just over a hundred pounds—and swung me in his arms like I was a little girl and said, "Vi, you're the best, honey," and then he kissed me straight on my mouth.

So that's the kind of guy Tub is, or was. Heart as warm as an in-ground tuber.

We drove home the rest of the way in silence. Round Mountain Road, North Branch, Old School. When we got to our track we left the Rabbit parked at the road and climbed up to our place on foot. Our house is way back in the woods in a place you can only get to with a truck in summer and a skimobile in winter. It's more like a collection of rooms tied together than a house—each covered in tar paper and whatever kind of siding came our way at the time—tin, plywood, pine. We don't have electricity and we don't have running water inside—just a hand pump well that sits out in the yard a ways. I guess that's why we never had kids, Tub and I, because we knew they never could have stood it, or liked it, like Tub and I do. Now there's only a moment or two here or there when I wonder—when I think about Tub being gone and what on earth is going to happen next—when I wonder what I might have done with a little squalling fish of a baby, milk squirting out of my two-bit breasts. But I don't wonder about it much.

The light was already half gone when we got to our place. "Goddamn chilly fall," Tub said, and when we got inside I lit a fire. Tub went outside to feed the horses, and I sat in front of the open door of the stove and felt the blood rush back into my fingers. The plastic that covers a broken pane flapped a little against its duct tape. That hole reminded me of other holes, and I tried not to think of the doctor's bills and the cracked valve somewhere in our Dodge or the two broken panes of glass in our kitchen windows. Forty-seven years ago I stood in Tub's mother's kitchen in a cotton dress with Tub's hand in mind while Minister Oley said something about the good times and the bad, and I thought about that then: the good and the bad.

I heard Tub coming in from the barn and put some canned beans with ham on the stove and added water. I helped him get his boots off at the door and poured us each a half glass of whiskey.

"Every man needs a little pleasure," I said. We ate our soup and pulled out the deck of cards. We sat by the window listening to the wind howling through the trees and watching the snow, just beginning to come down big and flat as coins. When the whiskey started to make its way into Tub's blood he grinned at me again with his charming ten-tooth smile and that sparkle came back into his blue eyes and his live heart and then he was the boy I knew again and he was the man that some nights, under the covers, still rolled over toward me and touched my body in the old way that is as familiar as pine pitch or hot water, the man who I still love and who I knew, those forty-seven years ago, I would love forever.

"Perty as a shooting star," he said to me across the table.

I just grinned and showed him my pair of tens.

"Pair of jacks," Tub said, and put his hand down on the table with a thwack.

"Goddamn," I said.

It was dark then, so I got up and lit the kerosene lantern and brought it over to the table so we could see our cards better. My Tub, he was always winning. He looked at me, his face hot and flush. Our house was warm from the stove and our blood from the whiskey. Outside we could just barely make out the spots of snow coming down onto the ground below.

"Goddamn snow," Tub said, looking out the window, and I thought about how when we died no doubt someone would tear down our collection of rooms and build a nice big house, like all the other ones going up around these hills. But I didn't care. If you learn one thing working with trees and woods and animals your whole life, it's that something's got to die in order for something new to grow. I thought of a couple of old stumps out in the woods, rotting and turning to dirt and making fertile ground.

"Goddamn winter," I said. We grinned at each other. And then Tub's grin turned into something different, some kind of grimace, and a look of terror flew across his eyes, and I thought again of those love birds up in the hemlock trees above his dead folks' stones, and I thought of them taking off, black against that blue-gray sky, and then Tub reached out toward me grasping for my hand, and I gave it to him, and that's when I realized Tub was dying. It was the quickest death I'd ever seen, quicker than any of the animals I'd seen die, and I'd seen plenty. I dragged him over to the rug on the floor—not easy, you know, Tub was big, and I'm small—and I curled up next to him as he heaved his last breaths, and then as his blood cooled, and I spent the night like that, with my Tub, there in our house, holding on tight, watching it snow. And now it's just me. And the horses. And the winter. And we're getting by. And everything I thought that night about stumps and forever is true. Did you write that part down?

11

THE WOMEN WHERE I'M FROM

My mother calls to tell me the farm is falling apart: fields overgrown with sumac, barn windows broken, the kitchen roof leaking water. She tells me her truck hasn't started for a month, the veggie garden is standing water, and the one remaining goat is too old to milk and too sweet to kill. She laughs, takes a drag on her cigarette. "And Hannah baby," she says. "I've got cancer. Breast."

"Jesus Christ," I say. I'm at the kitchen sink in my apartment in Seattle, overlooking a Chinese restaurant and a biker café. She says it's no big deal—the fixable kind—but that there are buckets of water scattered around the kitchen floor she just can't keep up with. So like that I buy a plane ticket home.

My rental car passes fields, trees, double-wides, barns. Ten years ago I left Vicksburg for art school, and I've only been back a few times since. I live with Matthew, a photographer with a trust fund, in a little apartment overlooking the bay. I work as a receptionist at a graphic design firm; late nights I drink too much Maker's Mark alongside him and watch movies set in rural places like this one. Now I turn left onto Stark Road, right onto Fox, past Silver Creek, past a barn with a slipping roof-tin, a field full of abandoned cars, a farmhouse surrounded by rust-pocked pastel trailers.

"What are the women where you're from like?" Matthew asked last night as I sat on our bed stuffing clothes into a bag. He took off his Clark Kent glasses and gleaned me with his clear, dark eyes. "You don't say much about your mother." He is gentle, soft-fingered, in love.

"I don't know. Stubborn. Why?"

He smiled. Kissed my bare foot. "Still trying to figure you out."

I laughed. Shifted my foot away.

At dusk I pull into my mother's driveway. Five years and the house looks the same: the large gray frame, slipping clapboards, sagging roof, a ghost surrounded by various outbuildings and barns. Her flower gardens are, as always, wild and bright and unkempt: William Baffin roses climbing up the porch rungs, daylily and Echinacea and phlox spilling out into the yard. But I take a deep breath when I see my mother. She stands barefoot in the wash of evening porch light in blue jeans and a gray silk dress peppered with holes. Her silver hair falls limp to her waist, her collarbones jut beneath her skin, her eyes are ringed by sockets of blue. At the edge of the porch we reach toward each other for a hug and her smell is overwhelmingly familiar—goat and the nutty tang of sweat and the rosewater she mists her face with—but there is another smell too: of sickness, or medicine, or both.

"Hi, Joan," I whisper into the crook of her neck.

"Hi, baby," she says, squeezing the skin of my arm, and I think, *I'm home,* and *Sweet Jesus. I'd rather be anywhere else but here.*

We eat dinner on the porch: bowls of pasta, Mason jars of red wine.

"Doctor's orders?" I say, nodding toward the wine.

My mother laughs. Shrugs her shoulders. The porch, like the rest of the house, is a mess: newspapers and books and cast-off sweaters coating every surface. She sits in a vinyl-covered glider; I sit in the lemon-colored two-hundred-year-old rocker she nursed me in until I was five.

My mother puts her bowl down and picks up a pack of American Spirits. "Mind?"

"Of course."

"Too bad," she says, winking at me. "My evening ritual." She lights a cigarette, closes her eyes, leans back into her chair, and starts talking. She says she's been ripped off twice this year. Two months ago, she tells me, a young man wandered up the driveway looking for a place to stay, so she gave him a sleeping bag and offered him the hayloft; in the morning she discovered the sleeping bag and the cash from her wallet were gone. "Asshole," she says, then tips her head back and laughs.

I'm not surprised—it's the story of her life. "Where'd you leave the wallet?"

I don't ask if she slept with him. The air is humid and smells of cut grass. I think of running across these fields when I was nine, trying to avoid the sound of my mother's boyfriend-at-the-time Kenny's guitar strumming incessant Steely Dan tunes. I think of how I had hoped then she would follow after me, throw her arms around me, ask about my sadness, and how she did not.

"What? Oh. It was in the car."

"And the second time?"

"Tools from the barn."

She tells another story: two weeks ago her Saab broke down on her way home from skinny-dipping at Sunset Lake. She had nothing on but a wet, see-through cotton dress. She giggles, snorts a little. "I had to stand by the side of the road like that with my thumb out until Joe Maise's young son—you know, the cute farmer who lives up the road—came by and picked me up." Again she laughs, tosses her thinning hair over her shoulder.

I don't laugh. I picture her thin body under translucent cotton by the side of the road, gray hair plastered to her scalp, and wonder what the young farmer thought as my mother climbed into his truck. I imagine him turning away, kindly.

She takes a drag of her cigarette and looks toward the pale sky that hovers above the dark field and the even darker line of trees, then reaches over and takes my hand in hers and squeezes it. She's lived here for forty years, the last ten of those more or less alone. "So. Hannah baby. You're home."

"Yes."

She turns toward me and smiles. "Pertier than ever."

"Thank you," I say, returning her gaze, but really in this light it's my mother who suddenly appears more beautiful than ever: as if this thinning is paring her down to her essential features, which have always been more classic than mine: Katharine Hepburn amidst the falling-in house and overgrown fields. *Grey Gardens* amidst the pines. The light in her eyes is dim, the rings around them dark as river stones.

"I'm glad you're back," she says, closing her eyes. Mosquitoes swarm the porch light; she slips a sweatshirt over her head that says RODEO BAR in pink faded letters.

"Me too," I say, looking down at my hands, down at my boots. "Me too."

The Stonewall Tavern sits tucked between trees at the edge of Route 100. I push the door open, and a cloud of music and smoke drifts past me. "No way! I can't believe you're back in town for real! This is so goddamn *cool*," my oldest friend, Kristy, calls out from behind the bar, her arms raised toward me.

"Yes it is," I say, smiling and leaning across the counter for a hug. She smells like jasmine and roses, and her smile is a beam of sunlight amidst the dark paneled walls of the room.

"So. What's the Wild West like?" she asks. She has changed little on the outside since we were eighteen: radiant dark skin, an electric smile, a tattoo of a swallow on her left arm, a twining rose on her right. I glance up at the taxidermied bobcat strung to the wall, its yellow eyes boring holes through the room.

"It's good. Badass and good."

"I can't wait to hear all about it."

"Yeah," I say. "Sometime." Though I wonder how I'll sum it up to this friend who has never lived anywhere but here: the vegan strip clubs popping up in my neighborhood, Matthew's unpeopled and pristine landscapes—full of romanticism and yearning. When we were twelve Kristy's dad, Trevor, killed himself by jumping off an interstate bridge into the shallow waters of Silver Creek. I spent that night on the floor next to her bed; our lives were once as entwined as fence post and honeysuckle. Now she still lives with her mom, Annie, down the hill from my mother's farm in a blue double-wide and tends bar and has never left this town, a stone's throw from Boston, or New York, or numerous other places she could have fled to, for any substantial amount of time. What is it, this tether?

"Nice to see your radiant face, Kristy," I say, placing my hand on her silver-ring-studded fingers atop the well-loved wood of the bar. She squeezes my hand and grins and hands me a shot of Maker's Mark.

I take a sip and glance around at the other people in the bar: Jason Dewey and Brian Cole, boys I knew in high school who are no longer boys. Jason was in Iraq for a while with the National Guard, I've been told. I'm glad he came back alive. I nod to them and they nod back. *Goat woman*, they, and others, called my mother. *Stinking rich*, they said loud enough for me to hear. They all knew she was a surgeon's daughter from elsewhere. "Jason," Kristy whispers to me over the counter, "is married to Tammy Bates now, and Brian has a kid with Liz Clay." I nod. When I left home it was breathing easy for the first time.

I finish my drink and order another and watch the dance Kristy puts on there behind the counter: all swivels and hips and flicks of the wrist. She leans her elbows on the bar and puts her head close to mine. "I heard about Joan. Being sick."

I nod. "I think she'll be okay."

"I know she will," she says, and squeezes my hand. I squeeze hers back and think of my mother's collapsing house and thinning body, of how she has made her mistakes—loser men, loneliness, drink—with such unfaltering surety, it shakes my mind. I think of Kristy's mom, Annie, in her blue double-wide, addicted to opiates and her occasional bouts with heroin.

"Hey, Han," Kristy says.

"Yeah?"

"Let's be hippies this summer."

I laugh. It's an old joke. We spent whole summers in my mother's dresses.

"Yes, let's," I say, smiling.

She squeezes my elbow. "Man, we are going to have a *ball*."

"Yes, we are," I say quietly. "We sure as hell are."

My mother sits at the upright piano playing one-handed Bach; in her other hand she holds a jar of wine. She tips her head back toward me as I approach and kisses my cheek. Her lips are stained; her breath, like mine, is all fermentation. Photos hang on the wall above the piano: my mother naked with a hoe in the garden; my mother pressing apples in front of the barn; twenty hippies square dancing in the south-facing field. For a while ten or more people lived here, and their parties were infamous. Friends of friends came, driving north from Boston and New York to press apples and pitch hay and shovel shit. My father was one of them. Which one, I don't know. There are pictures of me, too: long-haired and half naked, running through grass; flying through the air on a swing hung from the rafters of the barn; clutching an Araucana bantam to my breast and laughing. The commune was over by then; it was just me and her. Still: the girl in the photos looks too impossibly uninhibited and at home in these fields to be me. My legs streaks of muscle, my hair: sunlight. When did I change?

My mother stops playing and looks up. "Hey, Hannah," she says. Candlelight flickers across her face.

"Yeah."

"You remember that cat I saw? The catamount?"

"Yeah."

"I think it's around again."

When I was twelve she swore she saw a catamount. She was standing at the far end of the field fixing a spot in the electric fence when she felt the presence of something and turned. There it was at the edge of the woods, twenty feet away amidst the blackberries and pin cherries, standing stock-still, looking right at her. *Big as a Saint Bernard, quivering brown fur and electric brown eyes,* she told me that day when I got off the bus, the thin bones in her hands liquid with excitement.

It was the age when I began to fall out of love with her. Twelve: I so desperately wanted something other.

"There are sightings, you know," she says now. Her eyes have that same glint of light from seventeen years ago. "Those assholes at Fish and Game don't believe it, but people are seeing them."

The officials said it must have been something else—a large bobcat or a Canadian lynx, that catamounts hadn't populated these woods since the 1880s, but she got a book out of the library and showed me pictures of the Eastern catamount. *That's what it was,* she said. *That and none other.* She tore out the picture of the *puma*

concolor and tacked it to our kitchen door. Eastern catamount. Puma. Cougar. Mountain lion.

"That would be cool, if it's back around," I say, unbe-
lieving.

"Yes," she says, returning to her one-handed Bach. I
climb the stairs to my old room: west-facing drafty windows, low eaves, ancient wallpaper covered in little blue
ships sailing across a choppy sea. A few of my old things
are here: piles of artwork, boxes of journals, books. I slip
between the thin flannel sheets and think of that fantasti-
cal cat prowling, of my mother downstairs, drunk at the
piano. On the wall above my bed are posters of Joan Jett,
Patti Smith, and Nina Simone. *This,* I would say to Matthew, were he to ask me now. My head spins; the wallpaper blurs; the little ships take flight into air. *This is what
the women are like where I am from.*

I wake early, make coffee, and start cleaning the house. I
clear clothes and books and newspapers off the kitchen
table, run dust rags over the counters, load empty wine
bottles from the pantry into the back of my mother's
Saab.

At ten she comes in from the screen porch where she
sleeps during the summer. She brushes her hair away
from her face and looks around. "My God!" she yelps.
"An angel descended on me." She puts her arms around
my shoulders and kisses me on the cheek, her breath stale

and her lips still stained with wine. "Ay," she says. "And I need coffee."

I make her coffee and eggs and think of telling her that she should shower—I can smell her from where I stand—but don't. I sit down opposite her. "Tell me," I say.

"What?" She sips her coffee, her eyes darting from surface to surface.

"You're sick."

"No. Not sick. Not sick yet. Hannah baby . . ."

"Yes?"

She looks at me now, her eyes steady. "You don't have to take care of me. That isn't why I wanted you to come back."

"I know."

She sips her coffee and stares out the window toward the barn. "I just wanted you to come back."

"I know," I say. "I know."

"So long as you know. Because life is still all honey. All honey."

"Okay," I say. I don't meet her eyes.

I walk across the field and into the woods to the old Stark cemetery. In grade school Kristy and I used to come here to trace the names of women and children etched into the stones: Zipporah, Constance, Faith, Desire—her relatives, distantly, from two hundred years ago. Later, in middle school, we would come to the same spot and pretend we

were making out with boys: lay our bodies on the rotting leaves and wet moss, close our eyes, and imagine doe-
eyed, sweet, and handsome boys leaning over our faces,
touching our limbs, saying our names out loud. *Kristy.*
Hannah. Kristy. Hannah.

Today trillium blooms amidst the twisted, toothlike
stones that heave out of the leaves and dirt. I lie down like
Kristy and I used to do, close my eyes, and feel the sun on
my face. Constance, Faith, Desire? Matthew wants me to
bring him here, wants to meet my mother, wants to know
and draw the shape of these fields. Matthew: a kind-
hearted boy from the suburbs of Minneapolis. "You're
slippery," he said before I left, rubbing his thumb down
my spine, his eyes cloaked in sadness.

I said, "There are two worlds I won't ever belong to.
Home or any other."

He smiled, blinked: utterly confused.

The next day I follow my mother out to the barn to feed
Stella, the twenty-year-old goat with phosphorescent
green eyes, a long beard, and splayed bottom teeth. "Ugly,
huh?" my mother says, grinning.

Blaaat, Stella replies.

My mother scratches the fur beneath Stella's chin, feeds
her raisins from her palm. "I want to leave this world like
you," she half mutters to the goat, so quiet I can barely hear.
"Not in a fucking white gown. Not with my tits cut off.

Stella baby," she says, scratching the goat's chin again, and Stella butts her head into my mother's breast, and I think how this goat has taken the place of love and friendship and family. "You know how to go, don't you," she whispers into the floppy, mottled ear. "You know how to go."

She turns to me. "Know what the Kennedy Center's motto is?"

"No."

"*I look forward to an America which will not be afraid of grace or beauty. JFK said that. Isn't that lovely?*"

"Yes," I say, trailing, as always, the roller coaster of her mind. "Yes, it is." But really what I want to know is how long I am here for, and how to fix her roof, and her body, and her mind.

"What about the roof?" I ask.

My mother turns from me and walks out the door. "Oh, that," she calls out behind her. "Can wait."

A man leans against the bar next to me and orders an Otter Creek. His arms are tan below the sleeve of his T-shirt; thinning brown hair dips into his eyes. He pays Kristy for the drink, then turns to me. "Hannah, right?"

"Yes." I don't recognize this face; his left eye wanders slightly upward.

"Jesse Maise. From the farm down the road."

Jesse. I haven't seen him in fifteen years or more; I'm surprised how old he looks, how broken, how kind. "Oh, right. Hi." A pale, thick scar runs from halfway up his cheekbone to the corner of his eye.

He nods and rubs his beer glass with his thumb. "Bet your mother's happy to have you back."

"Yes," I say, thinking of her Saab broken down by the side of the road, of her wet cotton dress, of Jesse, it must have been, in his truck, reluctantly pulling over.

"She doing all right?" he asks.

"Yes. Thanks. She's fine."

"Not too many goats left, it doesn't look like."

"No. Just one."

"I always thought she was cool shit—doing it all herself like that."

I smile, surprised. I didn't imagine Jesse thought anything of my mother, other than different, or strange. "She is. She is cool shit."

"Thought all hippies were as pretty and independent as her." He laughs. "In college I found out they weren't."

I can't help but laugh too. "Cheers to her, then," he says, reaching his glass toward mine, and I raise my arm, and the glass clinks, and I follow him with my eyes as he walks back to a table in the corner below that cat's yellow eyes.

Kristy nudges my arm. "Sweet, huh?" I nod. She leans in closer, her voice a near whisper. "His daughter died—drowned—a few years ago. His wife left."

"Oh," I say. I can picture Jesse and his older brother, Clem, standing at the edge of a pond with BB guns, aiming at frogs. I can see Jesse—blond, scrawny, quiet—at the back of the bus, picking at scabs. I hadn't thought of him in a long time.

But I think about him that night back in my room. I think of that wandering blue eye and that mysterious scar and that loss; I think about letting him touch me like he touches the other things that belong to this place: tractors, fences, barn doors, cows. I think about my mother and death and fear and abandon. And I think of Matthew, sweet Matthew, who has left two messages on my phone, checking in. I leave a message when I know he's at work, promising I'll call soon. I pick a book off my old bookshelf and flip through the pages: Milan Kundera's *The Unbearable Lightness of Being*. It was my favorite. Sabina and her brazen solitude.

I drive my mother to her appointment: forty minutes by interstate. Her twenty-year-old Saab smells like mildew and cigarettes and the lemon air freshener that hangs from the rearview mirror. We listen to tapes she has kicking around on the floor of the car: Al Green, the Sex Pistols, Dolly Parton. The Saab shimmies as soon as we hit sixty, so I drive fifty-nine, the windows rolled down, my mother's seat tilted back and her gray hair whipping this way and that in the wind.

The oncologist with the bleached-tooth grin tells us he has scheduled radiation to start two weeks from now, but that nothing is cut-and-dried here. He looks at my

mother, then at me. "A mastectomy is possible," he says
nervously. Then adds, "Likely." He tells us that the key
to success is lifestyle and attitude. He says it twice, looking again into my mother's eyes, then mine. His eyes
betray his words, spill faithlessness. I think of her overflowing ashtrays and overgrown fields and dripping roof
and dying goat and drying-up inheritance. My mother
blinks and smiles and says, "Of course," and heads for
the door. On the way home she leans back on the head-
rest and closes her eyes. After a while she reaches across
the seat and touches my thigh. "You happy doing what
you're doing, baby?"

I look in the rearview mirror. "I don't know."

"Why not?"

"Too ornery." She opens her eyes then and we both
smile. But I feel something rise in my throat that is salty
and bitter, reeking of fear.

My mother roots around on the floor, then pulls up
a tape and pops it in. The Flying Burrito Brothers start
to sing "Hickory Wind." She pulls the visor down and
closes her eyes.

I drive home thinking about Gram Parsons' body in
an outrageous embroidered suit burning up in the desert of Southern California, about the strange ways we
choose to die. I think about the reckless beauty of my
mother's life compared with my small rooms and the art
I haven't made. At the next exit I pull off the blacktop

and take the back roads—gravel that follows Silver Creek and meanders past houses I've slept in, fields I've gotten drunk in, swimming holes where I've skinny-dipped or gotten stoned. These places that flicker with memory and strange grief and misrememberings.

They make me lose track of time; the days slip into one another. I've been here a week and a half, or two. My office has told me to take my time, but I still haven't bought a return ticket. How long is too long?

I drive to Indian Love Call to meet Kristy. It's on Silver Creek, over the bridge and a pull-off to the right. Seventeen years ago Kristy's dad died two miles downstream; now she sits on a log with a six-pack of wine coolers by her side. We roll our pants up, dip our toes into the cold water, open two bottles, and lean our faces and shoulders back to catch the sun.

"What do you think it feels like to be in love?" Kristy asks.

I feel the pores of my face expand, my skin open like a flower.

"I mean do you think you're in love with that guy in Seattle?" Kristy makes circles in the sand with her middle finger. I don't respond.

"I think I'm in love with Dylan Pial. He's in love with me," she says. I'm quiet. I remember Dylan from high school. Part Abenaki, part French, I think. Kind eyes.

"I think that men either idealize you or need you," I

say with my eyes closed, thinking of my mother's long string of boyfriends: the guitar player, an English teacher who grew pot in the basement, a motorcycle mechanic with a wife in New Hampshire. "It's one or the other."

Kristy nods. "I think he needs me." She has been in love many times; it's a knack she has.

"Infatuation," I say. "You need some of that. Keep them at a good arm's length."

"And make offhand comments about penis size," Kristy says, her chipped front tooth flashing in the sun. "To keep them guessing."

We laugh and sip our coolers and tip our shoulders back. Upstream, kids wade in the shallow pools, and below us the creek widens out over smooth rock. I dig my bare toes and heels into the sand.

"No, but for real," Kristy says. "I think he might be the one." She stares off at those kids, laughing and splashing.

"I have no idea about love, Kristy," I say. A racket of sparrows takes flight in my chest. They open their mouths, but no sound comes out. "I have no fucking clue about love."

My mother and I eat dinner on the porch: tuna and greens from the garden. She's missed all her scheduled appointments. Her answering machine fills with calls from doctors.

"Tell me something cool," she says.

"A starfish can turn itself inside out."

My mother grins. "Really? That's magnificent. But I was actually thinking something more personal."

I look at the woods, at the field, at my hands. "It's good to be here."

"Oh." She glances at me from under her furrowed brow. "I thought you might hate it here."

"How could I?" I look across the fields at the barns and the gardens and the ochre shadows of the trees. At the bottom of the hill I can see the roof of Kristy's double-wide, the tin roof glaring white with sun. Inside, her mom, I know, is drinking coffee and watching reruns of *Twin Peaks*. I don't hate it here; I hate what happens to me when I am here. I hate the way it draws me in. The way it leads to nowhere but itself. The way everyone and everything is connected and a person cannot be free. "It's too beautiful to hate it here," I say.

My mother laughs. "Yes," she says. "Yes it is. Why do you think I've stuck around all these years?" She sets her jar down and closes her eyes. After a while she drifts into sleep. Her body trembles once, her lips open. I take a moth-eaten wool blanket off my chair and lay it over her thin legs. I want to leave. I want to go home. I want to undress in front of Matthew to a slow song, a glass of cool bourbon in my hand. *Here,* I want to say. *Have me.*

My mother tells me she has something to show me. She leads me out the door and through the overgrown north pasture. From halfway across the field we can see a view of the Maise farm below us, its roof lines and gray hollows. "I saw Jesse the other day," I tell my mother.

She looks at me and grins. "Cute, no?"

"Cute as pie," I say.

She nods and looks in that direction. "You hear about his daughter?"

"A little."

"Three years old."

I feel my heart dive toward the grass, then deeper into the substrata of glacial till and bedrock.

"But let's not think about that now," she says, continuing uphill.

At the top of the pasture she stops and closes her eyes and tips her head back.

The field is quiet and still, the woods insulating the spot from the sounds of the trucks on Route 100.

"I like to come here," she says, "and pretend the world is going on without me. Like I'm a bit of nothing, nowhere."

"That's bullshit, Joan," I say quietly. "You're not nothing, nowhere." I want to be nothing like her. I want to be part of the world. And yet I think about the time I walked across the Golden Gate Bridge at midnight, drunk. I think of some of the ways I have slept with men: in search of obliteration as much as love.

She continues on toward the woods, and I follow. At the edge of the field she trails a stone wall into the trees and up a slope to a spot of revealed ledge. "Look," she says, pointing to a shallow cave in the rock face. She gets down on her hands and knees and roots around. "I found this a few days ago," she says, rubbing something between her fingers. I go to where she kneels and peer down at what she's holding: some fur, the color of coyote, or bobcat, or fox—I can't tell. It's the color of the twelve-point buck that hangs above the bar at the Stonewall. I look into the empty cave, and my skin breaks out with fear. It smells like piss and dank stone. "You think?" she asks.

"Think what?"

"Oh, come on. It's catamount. Cougar. Panther. I'm sure."

"Maybe. Or fox."

"Oh, Hannah."

"What?"

"When are you going to become a believer?" My mother's eyes are glistening.

"What do you mean?" There's unkindness in my voice. And hers.

"When are you going to believe in anything? In life or love or fucking wild cats?"

I don't respond.

"I'm sorry," she says, standing up and reaching her arms around my shoulders. Her face is flushed.

"Forgiven," I say, turning.

We walk back to the house in silence. When I get to

my room I find there is a new message on my phone from Matthew asking if I am okay, if Joan is all right, if he can come out to join me. I don't call him back. I tell myself I'll call later tonight. But instead I lie in bed and think about catamounts and cows and fireflies in fields and girls drowning. I think about what happens to a heart once it's known something like that, and where Jesse finds his company, and whether he believes in big cats, or love, or belonging.

"I want to mow the fields," I say the next day. My mother raises her eyebrows. When I was twelve I swore off shoveling stalls and stacking wood and weeding the garden; I told my mother I wanted to be a poet or a punk rocker, a Patti Smith of the world, and she bowed her head and said, "Fine."

Now she glances at the fifty-year-old rust-colored Farmall parked in the barn, then back at me. "You don't have to do that."

"I want to."

She looks out at the fields: two years of overgrowth tangled through them, blackberries and sumac invading the edges. "There's not really any point," she says.

"I want to."

She squints toward the tractor. "Okay. Climb on."

My mother stands below me and shouts instructions: how to lower and raise the cutter bar, how to work the clutch.

"You're crazy!" I shout at her, the tractor rattling and choking below me. "Doing all this by yourself."

"No choice, baby-girl. No choice," she yells back. I ram the gearshift into first, let up on the clutch, and the machine lurches into the field. I lower the bar; grass and sticks and leaves spurt out behind me. The engine buzzes in my ears, the steering wheel vibrates and makes the skin of my hands and arms itch, but I get into a rhythm. Back and forth, lower, raise, turn, lower, raise, turn, lower. At the edge of the field I glance into the woods and think of my mother fixing the fence that day, of what the feeling along her spine must have been. I think of some large and wild creature there, lurking, but all I see are squirrels, darting up and down the bark of trees. I finish the half-acre field. My legs ache and my arms and shoulders burn. Freckles have appeared everywhere.

"Well done!" my mother calls out, handing me a glass of ice water. I drink it fast, then stand on the porch and look out at what I've done; I'm disappointed to see the three other fields I haven't yet touched, but I'm proud, too, of that neat field saved for another year from the scrub that wants it. *The women where I'm from*, I think, *are crazy, yes, but also capable.*

A blue GMC pulls into the driveway. I walk out to meet him in the driveway.

"Jesse."

"Hi." He smiles, looks out at my mother's house and barn, rubs his face with the back of his hand. I have an urge to reach out and touch the scar, which looks both old and tender. "Wanted to see if I could help out with anything. Offer a hand."

"That's kind."

"Thought it might be about time." He takes off his hat, his thinning brown hair falling into his eyes. "Your mother doing all right?" I wonder what gossip is circulating now, and whether it's done in the name of sympathy or righteous satisfaction. My mother never made much of an effort to love her neighbors; why would they love her back?

"I guess. I think she's okay."

"Saw you up on the tractor." He looks at me; another smile flashes across his lips. I think of the boy on the back of the school bus and how this man is nothing like him.

"Yes. First time ever."

"Looked kind of natural."

I blush. "Thank you."

He looks at the barn and then at the gray clapboards of the house. He puts his hand on the door handle of his truck and pops it open. "Well. If you need anything, just say the word. No need to be puritan about asking for help."

"Thank you," I say again. And then, "Jesse."

"Yeah?"

"You want to go for a walk?"

He meets my eyes. "Sure."

We walk to the top of the field and back through the woods to the Stark cemetery. I tell him I've forgotten all the small details of this place, so he tells me the names of ferns we pass: maidenhair, ostrich, cinnamon, royal. I show him the names on the stones at the cemetery, and he smiles. "Not lighthearted folks, were they?"

"No."

He asks why I don't come home more often, and I tell him I envy the way he belongs to this place and it belongs to him.

He laughs. "That's one way of looking at it."

I tell him coming home involves opening my body to layers and ripples of memory and the confusion of belonging and not belonging and the dichotomy of both loving and hating my lonely and crazy mother.

He looks down at his hands, tugs on a piece of grass and uproots it. He looks at me like I am some skittering leaf, blowing this way and that in the wind. "You think you're the only one that feels confusion or pain?"

I think of rivers and lakes and deep-water wells and feel my heart freeze. "I'm so sorry," I say.

He looks down at his fingers. "It's okay."

We sit in silence for a while and then get up and walk the long way home around the edges of my mother's fields. Seeds fly everywhere: dandelion, milkweed, gold-enrod. Sunlight touches everything. Back at the house Jesse climbs into his truck and smiles through the open window. "Thank you," he says, and I nod, and stand there watching the back end of his pickup leave, my body tender to the point of breaking.

My mother sits on the glider after dinner and asks me for a jar of wine; I bring us each one and join her. Her eyes settle on the far horizon; waves of late-summer heat rise up and out of the field. She is eating little and her body thins daily; gray hairs fill the bath drain, drape across her pillow. I've called my office again. I may lose my job. Do I mind? The sugar maples are turning along the roadsides. Three times I've asked her about fixing the roof, and each time she's shrugged. "Before the fall," she says. "Before the fall."

I go inside, put Neil Young's *Rust Never Sleeps* on the record player and turn it up loud. When I step back onto the porch she is dancing in her chair—twirling her arms around her head, swishing her hair to the beat of Ralph Molina's drums. I down my wine and start dancing too; I swivel my hips and pout my lips and toss my head back and forth.

"Rock and *roll*," my mother says. She stands up, shimmies over to me, and reaches her arms out. "Dance with me, baby-girl?" she asks, so I put my arms around her bird-thin waist and we do, to "Pocahontas" and then

"Sail Away." Her breasts are small against my chest and unloved; I don't want her to lose them. When the music ends she tips her head back and laughs. "Coots!" she hollers. "Couple of crazy coots!"

I laugh too. The wine has gone straight to my heart. "Rooty-toot to the moon!" I call out, still holding my mother's body against mine. "Rooty-toot-toot to the frickin' moon."

At midnight Kristy and I meet in the field between our houses. We lie in the grass and lean back on our elbows; the dew-wet grass soaks into the butt of our jeans and the elbows of our sweaters. She tells me her mother hardly leaves the house anymore. She tells me she wants to get pregnant before it's too late, with Dylan.

"Really, babies?" I ask.

"Yes. Babies. Wouldn't I make a good mother? We're twenty-eight."

I look down at my grass- and dirt-stained hands. "Yes," I say to Kristy. "You would."

A stick snaps in the woods to our left, and I look into the dark rim of trees. A ripple of fear crosses my skin. "Don't you want kids?" Kristy asks.

"No," I say. A breeze, scented of river, shoots across the field, and I burrow deeper into my sweater. I can hear Kristy breathing. "You'll be a wonderful mom," I say, at last, my voice lost in my throat. "The best."

"I hope so," she says. "I hope."

I'm ten, maybe. I have a baby goat I've called my own—Penny—and three bantam hens who follow me everywhere I go. I put Penny in old cotton dresses I find in the attic; I put Penny in the cradle I find in the barn and rock her to sleep, singing. She sucks the bottle I give her. She looks into my eyes with devotion and love. She sucks my finger until it is tender and sore.

I walk down to the Maise farm. It's noon and I don't know why I'm walking that way; my feet lead me there. Jesse lives in a self-built house up the road, but he's at the farm all day; he greets me at the doorway of the barn and smiles. "Done here," he says, nodding toward the milk room. "Go somewhere?"

He drives the truck along the edge of a field to a place where the land slopes down to the creek, then rises up into a quilt of blue hills. It's hot in the truck. A drop of sweat runs down my side. "I have something to tell you," he says, cheeks reddening.

"Oh yeah?" I look out the window at the well-kept hillside, its lines straight, its fields clear with purpose. I imagine the story of a girl drowning, of where he was, or was not, at the time.

He wipes his upper lip on his sleeve, looks down at his hands. "Clem and I used to watch you and Kristy swimming down there." He nods toward the Silver Creek, where Kristy and I used to skinny-dip all summer, sure no one could see us. "Thought we'd died and gone to heaven."

I laugh, thinking of my gawky adolescent legs and tender, swelling breasts.

His cheeks explode in apple-colored splotches.

"I guess none of us grow up on an island," I say. Neither of us moves. Another drop of sweat glides down my spine.

Jesse takes his hat off, rubs his forehead, puts the hat back on. I reach across the truck seat and touch his hand. His palm is dry, callused, not sweaty like mine.

"Hey, Jesse." I look into his right eye, the one that looks like it is here, with me, not lost on other things.

"Yeah?"

"You ever seen a catamount around here?"

He smiles. "No. But I've heard them."

"So they're here."

"I've seen tracks. I've heard them."

I smile. I can't help it. "That will make Joan very happy. I'm going to tell her you're a believer."

"I've heard them, for sure," he says.

"Good," I say, and he smiles and starts the truck and drives me home.

I call Matthew that night from the top of the field, the only place my cell phone gets reception. He asks when I'm coming home, and I tell him I don't know; I tell him my mother still needs me. He asks again if he can come here, and I tell him no. He is silent. I think of his intelligent bookshelves, of how he prefers to make love in daylight, of how I always close my eyes.

I wake to a scream. It's a terrible sound, the music of nightmares. I run downstairs to the screen porch, but my mother's bed is empty, the covers tossed aside. I go to the door and am about to call out when I see her standing at the edge of the field, a lean silhouette bracing itself against the sky. I go closer; she is smiling, her eyes bright. "Cat," she whispers. "Bobcat. Or maybe my friend the catamount. The most horrible sound in the world, the sound of a woman being raped, or dying."

We stand there listening but the woods are silent. My heart is erratic, my cheeks hot with adrenaline.

"Why that scream?" I ask.

"Just their mating song," my mother says. "It sounds like they're dying, when in fact they're in love." She smiles then and we stand there in the dark for a while longer, waiting, the scent of cut hay coming from the field, the end of my mother's cigarette aglow, but the woods are quiet. A minute passes before I realize she is shaking.

"Joan. You're cold."

"No, not cold."

I put my arm around her. Her limbs are erratic, uncontainable.

"It's out there," she says, grinning. "Hannah baby, it's out there."

"I know, Joan. I know. I believe you."

"It's here. I can't believe it's fucking here."

"I know," I say. "I know." I put my arms around her. She is all bone and skin. The withered body of a girl. "I believe you," I say. "I believe."

I crawl into bed with her; I don't want to sleep alone. I reach for her hand under the sheets and hold it: thin, bird-like, a pocket of dry warmth.

"Hannah," she whispers.

"Yes."

"I'm happy here."

"Yes."

"Totally fucking happy here."

"I know."

"Grace and beauty."

"I know."

She sits up and lights a cigarette; the tip dances in the dark, streaking the way the lights of sparklers do. "Hannah," she says.

"Yes."

"I'm dying."

"No you're not."

"Yes. It's everywhere."

"No." I put my head in her lap and start to silently cry.

"Yes," she says, "but it's okay." She strokes my hair back from my face. "It's okay, baby-girl. Grace and beauty and life and love. It's okay."

"No," I say, sobs raking through my chest now, her thighs like the wooden carcass of a boat, taking me out to some farther water.

"It's okay," she whispers, my snot and tears all over the warm skin of her legs. "It's okay, baby. Okay."

My mother turns fifty-four the last week of August and wants a party. I invite Kristy and her mom, Annie, and Jesse: there is no one else. My mother opens up her closet and pulls out an old dress I haven't seen in twenty years—blue and green calico—and slips it over my shoulders. She slips a cream-colored one, dotted with holes, on herself, and hangs large turquoise-and-silver pendants from her ears. Her fingers brush my hair back away from my face. "Dashing," she says. "So lovable."

I shake my head and smile. We go out onto the porch, light candles, and wait.

At nine Kristy pulls up and leaps out of her truck. Her mom climbs out after her. This is rare: Annie leaving the house. Depression and medication and addiction, Kristy tells me, are fucking blue streaks through her family.

But Kristy's all light. "Hippies!" she calls out. "Am I dreaming?" She pulls out a bag of liquor and ice. "Juleps?"

I get a pitcher and jars from the kitchen and grab a handful of mint from where it grows wild at the edge of the porch.

Kristy pours; I pound. My mother takes a sip, coos with delight. "Ah! Taste of heaven."

"Thank you," Annie says, taking hers and seating herself in a rocker. She says it like she means it, but also like she is five feet under, the cool flame of her heart near drowning.

Jesse arrives, his hands tucked deep into the pockets of his jeans. Kristy pours him a glass, and my mother pats the seat next to her on the glider. "What I want," she says, smiling up at him, "is for you to sit next to me."

Jesse smiles. "Okay," he says, and sits in her chosen spot. He's shaved and brushed his hair back from his face with water and is wearing a button-down shirt made of soft cotton. My mother leans against his shoulder. She puts her nose against his arm and breathes in. "Ah," she says. "Goodness."

I think I can see his cheeks redden, but he stays there, kindly. Kristy tells us about her day at the Stonewall: ketchup on white shirts, Calvin McLean asleep on the bar, the details of her boss, Rita's, sex life. My mother giggles, laughs, coos. "Too much!" she calls out every few minutes. We get more drinks and listen to the crickets and the refrigerator buzzing and the distant growl of jake brakes on the highway. Annie's eyes settle on the field and stay there.

"Jesse," my mother says, "Hannah tells me you've heard the catamount."

"Yes, I think so. I've heard it. Seen tracks in the mud near the pond." My mother squeezes his arm, laughs. "Pour him another drink," she calls out, and I do.

Jesse takes a sip of his drink and turns to my mother. "You know, when I was a kid, I used to think you were some kind of witch."

My mother smiles, her body a carcass of blazing light. "Oh but I am. Reckless. Powerful. All-knowing." Her body curves and twines in the seat; she is back to her old dazzling ways.

But she's tired. She sets her drink down and closes her eyes. Annie finishes her drink, then excuses herself and steps off the porch into the dark. She's beautiful still, like Kristy, under those shadows where she lingers. She climbs back into her truck, and Kristy watches her body turning, those headlights.

I go into the living room and put on Emmylou Harris's *Pieces of the Sky.* We sit there facing the field listening to Emmylou's voice and pedal steel spilling out over the hillside, twining around the trees. A candle flickers, burns out. My mother falls asleep on Jesse's shoulder. Her body shudders. "You okay there?" I ask him.

He nods. "Fine."

"I haven't heard Joan's music in fifteen years," Kristy whispers. "Brings me back."

"Me too," I say. Bats flit in and out of the rafters, clouds lift, stars explode.

Jesse finishes his drink. "I should go," he says.

I prop a few pillows under my mother's head and help him slip out from under her. I walk with him to the door of his truck. He pauses for a moment and I touch his arm. "Thank you."

Jesse smiles. "Hillside of catamounts and beautiful women. Can't complain."

"No," I say, smiling. "Can't complain."

Later my mother rolls over and opens her eyes. "Girls," she says. "What time does Jesse drive down the hill from his place to the farm?"

"Four thirty."

"What time is it now?"

Kristy looks at her phone. "Midnight."

"Wake me at four fifteen?"

Kristy and I look at each other. "Yes."

We crouch in the weeds by the edge of the road. Kristy giggles; my mother burps. We are still part drunk; our knees and feet are soaked with dew. We hear a low rumble and see headlights streak across the trees and come down the road toward us.

"Now!" my mother calls out. We leap out of the ditch and start twirling in the road, our arms spinning above our heads.

"Hooo-hooo-hooo-hooo!" Kristy calls.

"Aaayeee!" my mother screeches. "Hee hee hee hee!"

"Creeaaww!" I say.

We are a cacophony of movement and wild sounds: cat,

owl, coyote, crow. The truck rolls to a stop in front of us, its headlights ablaze across our twirling hair and spinning limbs. We throw our arms and thrust our hips; we shake our legs and toss our heads. My mother is laughing so hard she can no longer call out; her howls transform into sobs; Kristy's have turned to hiccups. We are ridiculous, without music, dancing to our own desperate, uncensored rhythm. Then my mother straightens and slips her dress down off her shoulders. It falls to her waist and she bares her small breasts there in those headlights. Tears stream down her face, her neck, her chin.

I can just barely make out Jesse's face through the glass of the windshield: eyebrows raised, mouth half open: grief, astonishment, wonder.

"Now go!" my mother calls. We leap across the ditch and stumble out into the field. My mother collapses into the grass. Jesse flips his lights off, honks once, then rolls the truck down the road toward the farm.

"Joan," I say, turning her over onto my lap. I wipe her face with the sleeve of my dress. "Joan."

"Oh my God," she says, opening her eyes and spreading her arms. She looks up into our searching eyes. "Oh my good God," she says, smiling.

We lay my mother on her cot and sit facing the field. Kristy reaches over and squeezes my hand, and I squeeze hers back. The field turns blue with mist, and I think of that catamount, panther, mountain lion at the edge of the field and want, more than anything right now, to see it streak across the grass, to feel its defiant energy and impossibility and light, but the woods are quiet except for the buzz of crickets and the snapping of the electric fence where it touches grass.

"Wild," I say.

Kristy glances toward me. "Damn right," she says, grinning and closing her eyes.

The women where I'm from, that is. I'm telling Matthew in my mind. They're wild. Ridiculous. Alone in these houses. A cool breeze blows under the calico of my dress, licking my thighs. And me: in which house or field do I belong? The crickets are loud and everywhere. That same old, same old, same old love song.